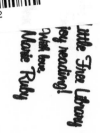

ENTRANCED BELOVED:

I SHALL NEVER LET YOU GO

BOOK FIVE OF THE *KASTEEL VREDERIC* SERIES

"Charmed and spellbound within a beloved's embrace is ambrosia or the immortality drink for the entranced beloved."

Ann Marie Ruby

Disclaimer:

This book ("***Entranced Beloved: I Shall Never Let You Go***") in no
way represents or endorses any religious, philosophical, political, or
scientific view. It has been written in good faith for people of all
cultures and beliefs. This book has been written in American English.
There may be minor variations in the spelling of names and dates due
to translations from Dutch or Indian provincial dialects, regional
languages, or minor discrepancies in historical records.

This is a work of fiction. Names, characters, places, and incidents are
the product of the author's imagination or are used fictitiously. Any
resemblance to actual persons, living or dead, is purely coincidental.
While the cities, towns, and villages are real, references to historical
events, real people, or real locations are used fictitiously.

Published in the United States of America, 2021.

ISBN-10: 0-578-31590-4

ISBN-13: 978-0-578-31590-4

DEDICATION

"Given vows tie generations of humans within a tree of life. This tree is neither created by birth nor death yet only through vows of the beyond."

Elixir of immortality is also known as the sweet drink that gifts one immortality. Yet what is immortality, or where does one find immortality are the questions saints have asked under the peace trees of life. The sweet magical immortality potion was sought yesterday, is sought today, and shall be sought even tomorrow.

I found my answers in this subject through my *Kasteel Vrederic* series. The immortality drink the whole world has been searching for lives within our own soul. We have traveled time through the pages of a history book. We have traveled to the moon as we watched Neil Armstrong set his feet on the moon. We have traveled through death and back as we watched scientists bring back to life so many human brothers and sisters through scientific discoveries. Yet today I want you all to travel through the pages of my *Kasteel Vrederic* series and realize for yourself what truly is the immortality drink of life.

I had asked this question myself and realized the answer was right here within my inner soul. For the answer was hidden within another question I had asked myself over the years. What is love? The mythological gods have sought the answer to the immortality serum as they knocked upon door after door. The religious saints too have sought the answer and had to satisfy themselves with the answers their hearts had eventually settled upon.

Ambrosia, the immortality drink of the Greek gods, was to be the gift of longevity to the consumers. So within my soul, I knew I had to find my own ambrosia. As I had written the *Kasteel Vrederic* series, I knew I had found my own ambrosia. Within the given vows of twin flames, I found my immortality serum. I unearthed this love within the promises made between an honorable soldier who had promised to keep his eyes on a castle even beyond death. I had recognized this immortality serum within the love and bond of a mother and her sons. I had comprehended the heartbeats can beat even beyond this mortal life through the bond of true love and lovers.

This elixir is also found within the given vows of two lovers who are not afraid of death as they say, "Reincarnation is a blessing if only you are mine." The inhabitants of Kasteel Vrederic have taught me what really is the elixir of life. I realized the promises made for one another between one another, even death could not be an obstacle. For don't let even death be an obstacle where and when you have your inner love.

Remember even the mythological gods searched for the elixir of immortality and could not figure it out. Yet you can have this immortality serum whenever your heart so desires. All you have to do is believe in this magical potion I call the elixir of immortality. This sweet passionate serum is the only serum you need to be alive and even in death, this elixir will live on eternally.

I have found this elixir through my magical inhabitants of Kasteel Vrederic. They taught me about this magical potion and it is only through their journey I too believe life is a blessing as long as you too believe in this magical potion I call love.

The sweet kiss on the lips that binds true soulmates in union throughout time is their ambrosia of life. The love and bond of a child and a mother are the immortality serum. The love and promises made between a grandfather and his beloved granddaughter are the only elixir a grandfather and his treasured granddaughter need throughout time.

Believe in true love and live life within this magical serum of love, for it shall keep you young eternally. Tonight as you hold on to your beloved know there within the eyes of your beloved lives your immortality serum.

I dedicate this enchanted, charming magical book to the magical immortality serum even the Greek gods had sought. I dedicate this book to the infinite kiss of passionate enchanted love. Remember all you need is the sweet magical

iv

kiss to live eternally throughout time through eternal love. The inhabitants of my magical Kasteel Vrederic believe even though life is mortal, love is immortal, so then love is the magical ambrosia, the elixir of immortality.

So all of you who are searching for the ambrosia of life don't really need to go and churn the oceans looking for this. For when you find your twin flame, the love potion that shall unite you toward your future generations is the only ambrosia you will need. It's hidden within your family tree.

Now you too can have a cup of ambrosia, the elixir, the immortality serum in your hands. All you need to do is travel with me across the pages of this magical book. Come take my hands and once again rejuvenate yourself with another infinite passionate love story I call,

Entranced Beloved: I Shall Never Let You Go.

TABLE OF CONTENTS

Dedication i

Prologue 1

Message From The Seventeenth Century: 13
Opa Help

Chapter One: 23
Vows From The Beyond Must Meet I Shall
Never Let You Go

Chapter Two: 38
Traveling Through The Tunnel Of Dreams

Chapter Three: 56
Traveling Through The Tunnel Of Light

Chapter Four: 73
The Seventeenth-Century Kasteel Vrederic

Chapter Five: 91
Margriete, Evermore Beloved,
I Shall Never Let You Go

Chapter Six: 108
Besieged Kasteel Vrederic

Chapter Seven: 125
The Invisible War

Chapter Eight: 143
Kasteel Vrederic Is Haunted

Chapter Nine: 163
Defeated By The Spirits Of Kasteel Vrederic

Chapter Ten: 186
Entry by Antonius Van Phillip

Conclusion: 217
Kasteel Vrederic Family Tree

The Inhabitants Of Entranced Beloved   233

Glossary   239

Message From The Author   244

About The Author   254

Books By The Author   259

PROLOGUE

Diary of Margriete "Rietje" Jacobus Peters

"A beloved grandfather stayed awake rocking his precious granddaughter to sleep, yet today a granddaughter only wishes she had not fallen asleep but could have held on to her grandfather for more framed memories."

Margriete "Rietje" Jacobus Peters for the first time encounters her entranced beloved knight, Sir Alexander van der Bijl, in front of the Lover's Lighthouse.

15th of December 1612,

In the front gardens of

Kasteel Vrederic,

Naarden, the Netherlands

P ouring rain danced with her partners, lightning and thunder, as she had put on a concert tonight, within the seventeenth-century Kasteel Vrederic, my home, my haven where I feel safe even within a stormy night. I have realized my home is my sacred blanket a child carries around for safety. I run around my home and never feel like I need anything other than my castle watching over me. My parents, the spirits of Kasteel Vrederic, are also always watching over me as my guiding angels. Yes I am the only person on this entire planet who can actually say this as my parents had died right after my birth. Yet they never left the home and became the famous spirits of our home.

For the love of a father who never got to hold his child, the daughter never left. For it was her words as she had said, "I shall never let you go, if only you were mine." Nevertheless they never saw one another in life yet as my mother was brought home in a coffin by my Opa, she never left the home. For even he had said, "I shall never let you go, if only you were mine."

3

My grandfather had placed his daughter in his chest after her death. Yet this family believes in infinite love not temporary. My father could not let his beloved twin flame go and had succumbed to his death as he was wounded in our Dutch revolutionary war.

We the citizens of the Netherlands still fight this war and hope we shall see a future where there will be no war but peace. I hope I can convince my grandparents so they would allow their only granddaughter to also do her part in this war zone, in order to bring peace upon the land and continue what my parents had tried to do.

I watched dawn come and bless my home as I knew I must first kiss my grandfather whom I call Opa and my grandmother whom I call Oma before I start my day. The love of my life is my Opa as he is the only one I want to see first in the morning and at night when I go to bed. My prayers of dawn and dusk are, may there never come a day in my life when I can't kiss my Opa and awaken to greet a new day or kiss Opa good night and be ready for a new dawn the next day. My prayer is, may a miracle take place and may my beloved Opa live eternally, and may he remember, "Opa's heart beats Rietje."

My name is Margriete "Rietje" Jacobus Peters. Today, I found this enchanted love potion-filled diary left for me by my very young and handsome Opa who is right now busy swinging on the swing with my Oma. I had made the miraculous swing with him and my great-uncle Bertelmeeus.

My Opa had written in his diaries never to end a story for a story never ends yet another one begins. So, I had tried to talk to my spirit, yes very real not see-through but very visible parents, yet invisible when they don't want me to ask them a question.

I asked them, "Papa, Mama. Can I go and join the war and try to help the soldiers? I would like to do my share, if I am allowed."

I knew they ignored me as I saw my grandparents smiling for they knew I was being ignored. I then said, "Papa, I want to look for an entranced beloved I can maybe fall in love with."

The whole Kasteel Vrederic trembled like a tremor. I then heard a loud bang and saw my soldier father standing in front of me as he said, "What did you say!"

The anger-filled voice got louder as he said again, "You want to go fishing for a suitor, in a war zone? Well young lady, you will do no such thing as long as I am still alive."

Then I saw Mama come in as she only watched Papa as he said, "Dead or alive, you will not even think of courting, do you hear me?"

My parents started to chase me as I said, "Mama, Papa, I heard you two, but I want to start my story and add it to Opa's diary."

My grandparents stood up as they held on to me and my Opa said, "Remember to write your own story. The diary is alive. All you have to do is tell her the truth, the whole truth, as then she will have your story written through words into another passionate and immortal love story, where you and your evermore beloved will recite to one another, 'I shall never let you go.'"

My Oma watched me and said, "My precious child, remember to stand in front of the Lover's Lighthouse and ask and seek whom your heart desires, if you are searching for your infinite twin flame. Only if your heart seeks the truth and knows the truth, and if the person standing by you is your beloved, then you both will see a couple appear in the lighthouse as this was your parents' unconditional gift of love left for you. This my dear is also my blessing left eternally for all true lovers as my daughter and her beloved Theunis will guard true lovers through this lighthouse for, ever after."

So, tonight I had stood in front of the Lover's Lighthouse and wished my eternally beloved finds me as I wanted to find him too. I prayed my country finds her freedom and maybe I will travel somewhere far to a fantasyland where my beloved will be waiting for me under the same skies, just maybe.

I was running impatiently as I knew my Oma wanted me to be in bed before dark. Nonetheless, I bumped into someone very hard as if he was made out of iron or steel. There in front of me was a very tall knight with a sword and his beautiful black horse by his side.

I asked him, "Who are you? Why have you entered my Kasteel Vrederic?"

He said, "I am Alexander van der Bijl, a knight and great-grandnephew of Sir Krijn van der Bijl. I was personally asked by the great knight to keep an eye on your castle, as it was a promise given by my great-granduncle to your grandfather. The protection will include you too as you are an inhabitant of this castle, I believe. If not, then I will personally escort you out of here."

As the moon shined above Kasteel Vrederic in the moonlit courtyard, I saw a very attractive man, six feet, four inches tall, with black hair and green eyes, dressed in a knight's attire. He stood in front of me and wanted to escort me out of my castle. Yet I knew I could escort him out of Kasteel Vrederic as I might be a woman but I am a trained swordswoman, as I was trained by Sir Krijn himself.

I first finished my prayers in front of the lighthouse. As he too watched me, he did the same gesture as if he too prayed. Then he watched me as I screamed, "Opa! Oma! Who is this very rude guy?"

Oh yes, the love stories within Kasteel Vrederic never end, as if you can't go and find your beloved then just maybe he will come to you. Do you believe in true love stories? I believe love stories never end as my love story begins right here. Charmed and spellbound by the first sight of a stranger, I named my diary as my beloved Opa had magically known or maybe seen, *Entranced Beloved: I Shall Never Let You Go*.

The end, no, I should say the beginning.

Signed,

Margriete "Rietje" Jacobus Peters

ENTRANCED BELOVED: I SHALL NEVER LET YOU GO

Spellbound and charmed

By a stranger.

A knight in shining armor,

Came upon my courtyard.

Under the mystical moonlight,

I saw him,

Yet it felt as if I knew him from

The inner court

Of my soul.

He entranced me

As he said,

The inhabitants of my castle,

He will protect with his life

Even though he knew not,

I too am a member of this castle.

Enchanted by his magical oath,

I knew in front of my eyes stood,

My knight in shining armor.

So I too vowed and made a promise,

ENTRANCED BELOVED:

I SHALL NEVER LET YOU GO.

Dear Beloved Sir Alexander van der Bijl,

This poem was written only for you. As I had given all my inner love to my Opa and my family, I did not know if I could even love any other soul. Yet when I saw you, I realized my love for you is very different than the love I have for my family, especially my Opa. Yet I knew as you stood in front of me the first time, it is then I realized, you too loved this nobleman, my Opa more than even your own life.

You had said if life ever gives you a chance, you would gladly become his personal warrior, his personal servant who only wants to serve him eternally. I know the feeling as I too have become my Opa's personal bodyguard eternally. That day, I also gave my mind, body, and soul to you as I knew you were my twin flame. I wanted to be with you and grow old with you. I prayed in front of the Lover's Lighthouse to have you as my entranced beloved eternally.

I know our love will only grow even beyond time. May our love story be an example of infinite love that unites a man and a woman into one complete love story. I pray this bond also is the immortality elixir of life through our children, grandchildren, and great-grandchildren. Through the infinite love of our family, this tree will grow infinitely. This family tree will be our family's immortality serum throughout time. As I am yours throughout infinity, I love you forever my entranced beloved.

I am your entranced beloved,

Rietje

MESSAGE FROM THE SEVENTEENTH CENTURY:

Opa Help

"Who does one call for help if the only person you turn to for everything in your life is no more?"

*As the seventeenth-century Kasteel Vrederic is invaded
by the enemies, Margriete "Rietje" Jacobus Peters
seeks help from the only place she knows she can ask.*

Seventeenth-century
War-torn
Kasteel Vrederic

ear Mama, Papa, and Opa,
The day is dark and dingy as today our home was invaded with the unjust warriors who only saw their country, not mine. They are blind to the innocent citizens of the land who only want to live in peace.

I am writing this letter to the spirits of Kasteel Vrederic, for help. Please Mama and Papa, help Opa and Oma, as today even I have been taken a prisoner. I have a few minutes before they will take away all of my belongings too. The Spanish army has taken our home as their hostage as they entered our castle by force.

Opa refused to hand over our home to them as their camp where they were going to keep all the prisoners captive. It seemed like without our permission they had started to bring in prisoners. Women and men who refused to accept their terms were being captured. Women and men were captured in the name of witchery as some were even to this day tried and falsely accused of witchcraft.

They called Opa a betrayer as Opa had rescued women who were wrongfully being hung at the gallows. Our home they wanted to prove is haunted and so they had forcefully entered saying they are only trying to get rid of the evil hauntings of the castle. Opa was shot from the back as he tried to rescue some young girls who were being captured as accused witches yet are being used as sex slaves. They shot him in the back somehow piercing his heart. Oma ran outside and she tried to stand in between Opa and the gunfire as he fell unconscious on the ground. They shot Oma multiple times as she too fell on the ground. Yet somehow she stood up and brought Opa inside.

Sir Alexander fought all day and all night against a huge army all by himself. I too joined him until we all fainted and fell. My brave Oma somehow with blood all over herself went outside and brought all of us inside. She hid us in a room behind the bookshelves which she said Opa had built as a safe house. I believe in miracles as you two are the biggest miracles in my life. However, today I ask you two to do something and save Opa and Oma. Please help. I must hide the diary in Opa's secret closet behind the library.

Sir Alexander is with me and he is trying to fight all by himself against a huge unjust army. Nevertheless he is outnumbered as he fights against an army of unjust Spaniards. I hope this letter written in my sacred diary reaches someone who will know what to do.

Opa, please hear my calls for I really need you today. Everyone keeps on saying you are no more, but I know you are just sleeping on your bed as Opa how could your heart not beat if my heart and Oma's heart still beat? You had told me to place all my thoughts and heart's desires into the diary you had gifted me.

You had promised this diary is magical and shall go to the person the diary should be with. The diary has her own mind and will. I believe in the words of my Opa, Jacobus van Vrederic, as I know for him, the spirits of Kasteel Vrederic will travel time and place. They will make sure my Opa receives my message.

The Spaniards could not find us in the hidden chamber and have made our home their campsite. They have come looking for Opa for they believe Opa had taken Papa as a prisoner as Papa was a soldier of the Spanish army who fell in love with a Dutch woman. They believe Mama had bewitched him as she was the daughter of Oma who they believe is a witch.

They also have decided I am a witch because I was raised by the spirits of Kasteel Vrederic and my Oma. They don't believe the story of how Opa had saved Oma. They are punishing Opa for this too.

I wanted to tell them the truth was written in Opa's diaries yet I did not want them to take the diaries away from us and erase the truth. So I hid the diaries and have risked our lives trying to hide them and all of us. I retold my Papa and

Mama's love story and how they both had passed away together. Yet my words found no ears who would listen to my words.

My Opa is lying in bed bleeding from a wound they had made. I know Oma will not survive as she was shot multiple times. Yet she is holding on to Opa and as if for him, she does not even care about her own pain. If Opa does die, she too will as she is bleeding a lot yet is crying only for Opa not herself. Oma is repeating nonstop and not even hearing any one of us, "How could your heart not beat if my heart still beats? You promised Jacobus we will always be together, then where are you?"

Today our family honor has become tarnished because we tried to save lives. The news of bread appearing at our home miraculously also is being investigated by these unjust goons as heretical crimes. Sir Alexander the warrior had arrived at our home in time, yet he was overcome by the mighty wrongful warriors who hunt down innocent women and men as their prey.

Today my Opa is bedridden as a victim of the unjust war, bleeding nonstop which I couldn't stop. My Oma is being held a prisoner and is fainting nonstop from crying for Opa. She is bleeding nonstop which I tried to heal but couldn't stop.

I only hope my heartbeats can call upon the one person my heart beats for. Please someone come and help convert our sadness-ridden horrific castle back into a home where our hearts beat for one another. I pray may my words not go in vain and may my words be heard by the beholder of my heartbeats. I know I had said all my life, "Opa's heart beats Rietje," however, today I want to say, "Opa, my heart beats your name."

Please help and don't let our family diaries end in vain. Somehow I know you still can hear me, as I still hear you say, "Opa's heart beats Rietje." Today as I don't have anyone else to go to, I only ask my Lord, may there be a miracle and may my letter reach Opa, wherever he is. Opa, I really need you now. Please don't desert me. Please somehow, Opa help.

Signed by,

Seventeenth-century

Margriete "Rietje" Jacobus Peters

CHAPTER ONE:

Vows From The Beyond Must Meet I Shall Never Let You Go

"A person travels to the future through reincarnation, then why could a person not travel to the past through dreams?"

Dr. Jacobus Vrederic van Phillip, standing in his family library, holding on to Margriete "Rietje" Jacobus Peters's diary, worried about the missing words in the blank pages.

K asteel Vrederic library in the twenty-first century. I am Jacobus Vrederic van Phillip, and this is the blank diary of my ancestor Margriete "Rietje" Jacobus Peters. I came upon the diary like a Christmas miracle.

It bothered me as I never got to read the diary before. These days though the diary was becoming blank and I wondered what was going on. So I decided to write in it, with hope of a miracle.

Maybe the author who had begun writing this would then finish it. Maybe she could write the conclusion chapter of her infinite love story, how it all had begun, and how it all ended with forever after. We all are descendants of this talented young woman. Yet today I wonder what would happen if the pages of her diary become blank? Like her blank pages, would my family too become dust and ashes?

As a physician, I do believe in miracles as even after science and all the efforts of a good physician, we all need a miracle once in a while. I have seen a lot of miracles being a son of the famous Kasteel Vrederic. I love my day job and the miracles of being able to save a life.

My job, however, is my second love as my first and last love is my mother. I had said to my mother at a very young age a phrase my ancestor Rietje had said to her Opa.

25

I had said, "Mama's heart beats Jacobus." Tonight I watched my baby nephew say to my mother, "Mama's heart beats Andries."

My baby brother is back again through the door of reincarnation. My mother believed in it and her faith brought him back to her. My brother and his wife never argued against it. For they too knew in their baby son was Andries, who had traveled through the door of reincarnation to be back within the arms of his grandmother whom he still calls, Big Mama.

Something just appeared today in front of my eyes as I opened Rietje's diary. I wanted to be sure this was not here last time I had read the diary. Was I hallucinating because I was sleepy or did a note actually come? I read this over and over again as it read, "Opa Help."

I called my mother and father and I saw my entire family come running like a wild whirlwind winter storm.

My father Erasmus van Phillip, a tall six-foot-five-inch European man with brown hair and pale complexion said, "Jacobus my son, what is it? Do you have a fever? Are you all right? Okay Anadhi, call the doctor now. My son is not answering, he must be in a state of shock or something."

Before I could speak, my very petite five-foot-four-inch, half-Indian and half-American mother who looks like an Indian goddess with black hair and olive-colored skin came running in. She said, "Everyone move and let me see my son. Jacobus don't you dare faint or else I will make sure you do faint from my screams. I just got back one son and now don't you dare go anywhere."

My brother Antonius van Phillip came running in as he then said, "Big brother don't you dare think of anything funny because I will follow you to wherever you go, because I will not allow the Grim Reaper to come anywhere near you even if he wants to. I will go first because I can't take any more of losing brothers or family members."

It was so strange as I wondered what had happened that my family members were all screaming and shouting at me. If I had not fainted, I definitely would faint from their screams. I realized I must have fallen asleep as I was trying to read Rietje's diary. I remember calling my parents and then all I can remember is shouting and screaming of family volunteers who wanted to take a ride on the boat of the Grim Reaper so I could escape death.

I watched my sister-in-law Katelijne Snaaijer and my nephew watching over me. She was my favorite patient. Always positive and a very wise woman who knew how to always bring joy and laughter into the rooms of all she entered. My sister she became as my mother refused to call her daughter-in-law but accepted her as a daughter.

I then realized I had not seen this side of Katelijne, a very positive European woman, five feet and seven inches tall with brown hair, scream and shout at me too. She said, "Big brother Jacobus, don't you dare make any plans to go on a ride with the Grim Reaper. I just got off of his boat after fighting with him with your help. I am holding on to Andries van Phillip, reincarnated, because of you. Don't you dare leave us, otherwise you will have me fighting to get back on the boat as your replacement, do you even hear me?"

I realized I was somehow transported to the sofa in the library. I wondered how they transported a six-foot-tall man like myself onto the sofa, I did not even want to know. I looked a lot like my father, with European pale white skin, a French beard, and brown hair. Yet everyone said I had my mother's shadow somehow.

I spoke for the first time as I knew if I didn't speak, the whole neighborhood would appear from the screams of my family members. I told them, "Everyone calm down. I must have fallen asleep as I did not sleep for days. Or the shock of a diary disappearing in front of my eyes has me confused. I only wonder if Rietje never was, then all of us too would be no more. It's strange but I am serious and am really worried. I received a letter from the seventeenth-century Rietje as I do believe I am the reincarnated form of the sixteenth-century Jacobus van Vrederic. I also can hear Rietje's calls."

No one said anything as all of them somehow became silent. I wondered if there was a stop button for my family as they all start at the same time and stop at the same time. I realized how much I too loved all of them. Yet my mind kept on going back to the seventeenth century where my beloved Rietje was calling me.

I told them, "It is like I can hear her calls. As if somewhere in my heart, there is a button that can't stop loving her. As if my heartbeats can hear her heartbeats. I know twin flames can hear one another, and my twin flame is Margriete. I will either find her and marry her or remain a bachelor for the rest of my life. Yet I can't explain how my heart beats for her. I feel like she is my granddaughter. It's strange and weird I know. But I can't explain it. I feel like my granddaughter is my entranced beloved I can't give up on, and Margriete is my evermore beloved."

I wanted to take a breather as I heard Papa say, "I know how it feels. It's like how I feel for Griet the spirit of Kasteel Vrederic. It is an oath I too made as I thought with God as my witness, I too will make sure you do marry

Margriete somehow. Then and only then, I will be able to bring back my granddaughter Griet van Jacobus, the forbidden daughter of Kasteel Vrederic, back home as the beloved daughter of my home. I only wish one day she too would know, this Opa's heart beats Griet."

It was then Mama said, "What is it that appeared in the diary Jacobus? Let's see what it is and we will make sure we get to the bottom of it. We should never forget we have the spirits of this castle watching over us. We shall call upon them for guidance. For where there is a will, there is always a way. It might be hard and even dangerous. Yet like I told all of you, we can all dream travel if only we are guided through the hands of the blessed spirits through the door of dreams. I have done it before and I shall guide all of you through it this time."

It was then I shared Rietje's letter that appeared in the diary. It was named, "Opa Help." After we all finished reading the letter, it was agreed upon we would all travel together if possible. We all asked Mama to guide and help us. As she is a dream psychic, I knew she would be able to.

She asked me, "Jacobus call upon the spirits of the castle as they are here only for you. I have watched them travel with you to even the hotel as we rescued Katelijne from there. I know they will answer your calls. For I always knew it was you whom they have followed even to the future for. They are protecting this family because of you. Yet today you must ask them to help you protect their only child who needs their intervention."

I watched at the door were waiting two very familiar spirits, my beloved couple, my daughter and son-in-law from my previous life. They watched me and in front of everyone, they became visible. Like living humans, they became visible, yet they were somewhat see-through. In front of everyone were standing the spirits of Kasteel Vrederic.

They introduced themselves as Griet in a clear form and voice said, "I am Griet van Jacobus and this is my beloved, my twin flame, my dear husband Theunis Peters. We have come here today as we need your help. Our only child is dying and must be saved with the intervention and help from her own future lineage. You all are her only help. You don't have to travel far for all of this is happening in this same castle."

She watched her husband as Theunis said, "Jacobus, it's amazing to see you again. This time I would want you to accompany us to the seventeenth century as time is strange and weird at times. For right now in the same room you all are standing, our child is fighting death. She is trying to communicate with someone as she knows her Opa in life, in death, or in the future can hear her. Through the door of dreams, you all can travel yet as we will hold on to all of you who travel, you shall all come back home safely. However, if Rietje dies, then all of this family shall be no more. It shall appear as if this family never was."

I told all of them, "Let's travel then and let's not be delayed for this journey will be to save our family lineage. So it must be done now. Now Theunis and Griet guide us and show the way to the past. Mama can also be our guide for she is the dream psychic who has been the one who has held our family together through dreams and reincarnation."

It was then Theunis said, "Okay everyone, now the two family diaries must unite for this journey. Through the door of reincarnation, you all traveled to the twenty-first century. Now through the door of dreams, you all must travel to the seventeenth century."

I told everyone, "It's time everyone we must liberate Margriete 'Rietje' Jacobus Peters from her captors and help her write the conclusion chapter in her sacred diary called *Entranced Beloved: I Shall Never Let You Go*. Now all the beholders of *Vows From The Beyond* must meet *I Shall Never Let You Go*."

I SHALL NEVER LET YOU GO

Family trees

Are planted across time,

For they begin in a garden

In the past.

The stories are written

In the family diaries.

Yet as time passes by

And the tides wash away,

The memories too fade away,

Before reaching other members

Of the same family

Across time and tide.

Yet if only each and all family members

Could write down

All the memories

In their blessed diaries,

It is then,

And only then,

The diaries

Would take you across time.

As that's how

The inhabitants of one diary,

Could then greet and meet

The inhabitants of

The other diary.

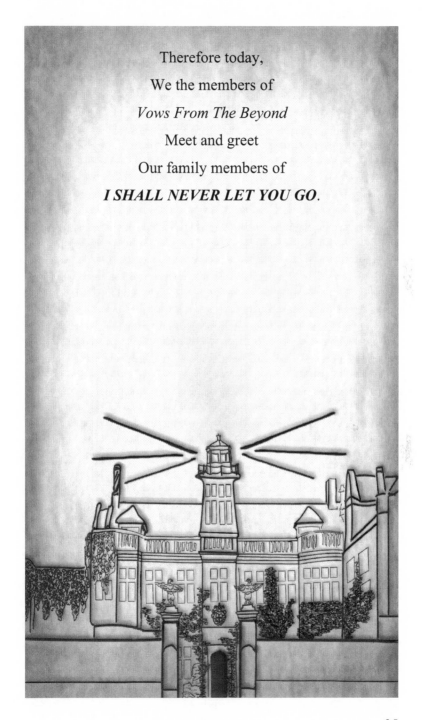

Therefore today,

We the members of

Vows From The Beyond

Meet and greet

Our family members of

I SHALL NEVER LET YOU GO.

My Dear Rietje,

Today I am going to introduce you to your family members who have kept their memories inscribed in their diaries called, *Vows From The Beyond*. I am blessed as I have traveled through both diaries and have created a bridge into both diaries through my lives lived. Yet today you too can travel through both as you only open your diary and read all the notes left from your family members of *Vows From The Beyond*.

For we are all blessed to have been able to read this amazing diary. I am writing in your diary as I know then you will not have a blank diary, but one that has been filled with love from your future generations' intercession. Write in the conclusion chapter my sweet granddaughter for then I shall read it in the future as your diary.

This is such a blessed diary that was only possible to be created through the bond of love and time. To the world and all of our future generations, this enchanted diary will be known as, *Entranced Beloved: I Shall Never Let You Go*.

With love and blessings from all of your family members of *Vows From The Beyond* and *I Shall Never Let You Go*, I am your Opa, the original diarist.

Your Opa,

Jacobus van Vrederic (sixteenth and seventeenth centuries)

Jacobus Vrederic van Phillip (twenty-first century)

CHAPTER TWO:

Traveling Through The Tunnel Of Dreams

"The door of dreams has brought people to open their eyes to religion. Today even science accepts the door of dreams. So today let's open the magical door through dreams and cross even time, if only you believe."

*Dr. Jacobus Vrederic van Phillip stands by the window
in the twenty-first century speaking to the spirits of
Kasteel Vrederic about his seventeenth-century
Margriete van Wijck.*

T
he trained medical doctor inside of my mind, body, and soul, was vibrating in fear as to what was happening in front of my eyes. The inexplicable truth of life and its happenings are just that, inexplicable. As a doctor, I work with science and miracles each and every day.

The storm brewing outside of my castle window brought back so many memories from my past life. I kept on seeing a very fragile woman standing near the same window I was standing by, shivering in the cold afraid of the furious storm brewing outside. Was she lonely tonight trying to remain brave? I kept on hearing her voice, my beloved twin flame Margriete's very shaky voice.

I asked in a very low whisper, "Is Margriete okay Theunis? Is she standing right here crying and asking why her heart still beats if my body from my previous life laid in bed lifeless?"

Theunis, my amazing traveling buddy and my son-in-law from my previous life seemed worried. I said to him, "You still look like you did centuries ago. You have not changed at all. You were worried about my then body leaving the Earth as I got shot, and now you are still here worried about my death again. Yet I am guessing this time, I did not make it."

Theunis laughed for a while and said, "In reincarnation, people forget the details yet remember only segments of their past life. How is it you remember even the small details? As if you have just traveled through the pages of a book into another book, yet with all of your past memories intact. Also answering your questions Jacobus, yes she is standing where you are standing right now. She is screaming and knocking her little hands out on the glass windows asking you the same question."

I knew I must control my inner feelings and become a man who has a firm heart, not a man with a soft heart, a man capable of calculating his feelings. I only wondered how do I achieve this goal? For I thought it was Margriete who had converted this iron-clad heart into a heart which did beat. I actually realized only after I touched Margriete so passionately after chasing her for days, I realized I too had inner feelings.

Nevertheless, all of my love and all of my feelings I had left behind with her. I had lost Margriete once and converted all my love into the love of an Opa. Now how do I learn to give up the three women who had made me into the man I became? My beloved wife Margriete, my beloved granddaughter Rietje, and my beloved daughter Griet, the spirit of Kasteel Vrederic, whom I never even held as a father.

The mysterious woman who could see much more than she would say, my mother, was silent. Strange to her character yet not at all strange to either one of us. We knew she just closes up when her paranormal psychic ability takes over. My mother never forecasts what she sees but waits for the end results.

She writes down everything she sees in her own diary of dreams and we all get to read it at the end after we all see her dreams in actuality. However, we all know she will intervene when she knows we must change our forecasted destiny. For she believes some dreams are shown as cautionary advice and so must be paid heed to.

My mother watched me and said, "My son I can hear your heart's calls even though you don't utter the words. I must warn you though, you must control your inner feelings for Margriete of the sixteenth and seventeenth centuries. She was the sixteenth and seventeenth-century Jacobus van Vrederic's wife and beloved. She does not belong to the twenty-first-century Jacobus Vrederic van Phillip. For your reincarnated Margriete will be waiting for you in the twenty-first century. Do not ever forget that or you will miss out on uniting with your twin flame in this life."

I watched my mother who knew me better than anyone else on this Earth and just laughed out loud. I only told her, "Mama's heart beats Jacobus."

She then watched me and said, "Yes my son, always and forever my heart beats my three sons exactly the same. Yet you must control yourself when you are in front of Margriete in the seventeenth century. For you cannot mess up anything over there. We just need to rescue Rietje and Sir Alexander van der Bijl. Then we come back home where I promise you will again have a chance at uniting with the twenty-first-century Margriete, if only you recognize her."

I watched my father as he smiled at her and said, "Anywhere, anytime sweetheart. He is my son and he will recognize her. I will make sure he does."

My brother Antonius said, "Oh yes Mama, I will make sure he does not fall for the older Margriete and falls for a woman his own age. Why would he anyway fall for our ancestor? Hey Jacobus, how could you even feel for a woman of the sixteenth century? I am going there to save my grandniece and her husband. That's all."

Katelijne said, "Your grandniece is Jacobus and Margriete's granddaughter. Even though it's from another lifetime, the feelings are still the same. At least I hope you too would have the same feelings for me in other lifetimes Antonius. I am now worried about it though."

I watched husbands and wives fight over my lost love life as I had to intervene. For even Mama and Papa started to question one another as Mama said, "Erasmus you knew me in other lifetimes, right? Now say it. Did you or did you not?"

Papa watched me and told Mama, "Sweetheart you know my answer, anywhere, anytime."

I watched the questions flying from one couple to another as I saw my daughter Griet in her spirit form laugh and say, "Papa is much stronger than all of you think. For Mama he became a lover, a husband, a father, and a beloved grandfather. I know for her he will again control all of his feelings. For he knows she is not his but belongs to the sixteenth and seventeenth-century Papa. Our secret phrase was, 'I shall never let you go, if only you were mine.'"

I told everyone, "I shall never let her go, as these will be my vows from the beyond in this life. For I shall travel time to save our granddaughter so therefore I shall be able to hold on to her in this life and repeat to her the same phrase, 'I shall never let you go.' For her I gained my feelings and it is time for only her I shall again place all my feelings locked up into my own heart. I shall feel like a son, a grandfather, and a brother, not like a lover or a husband."

My family members watched me and suddenly became quiet. I watched my spirit daughter from the sixteenth century pinch her husband and say something in his ears.

He then said, "How could I be of help as you all travel to the seventeenth century? It will be hard and your bodies will fall asleep in this room. So I do suggest maybe one of you remain here to monitor all of you. If you seem unsettled or are not waking up, the person only has to touch you and you will wake up. The person who touches you must be somehow related to you."

Everyone watched one another and wondered who should remain behind. No one wanted to be left alone as everyone wanted to be together. It was like everyone wanted to live or die together.

I told everyone, "Come on guys, someone must stay behind. I know Nani and Grandmother are too old and even if they are awake to awaken us, they will fall asleep and accompany us without even realizing. They sleepwalk and don't even realize they are both sleepwalking. So one of you must stay behind."

Papa said, "Not me, for I will not abandon my son in this life. I had done this in my other life and regret that even in this life. I will be with him even if that means I will be stuck in the seventeenth century."

Antonius started to say, "I won't be left behind, for I must make sure I bring my brother back with me, so I can become an uncle and have Griet as my niece in this life. Whatever I must do, I will."

Mama started to cry as she said, "If only I was with my son then in that life, my granddaughter would have lived to see her daughter Rietje get married. I will not let go of my husband or son in life or in death."

I listened to all of their reasons and knew no one would volunteer. So I asked Katelijne, "Would you as a member and a daughter of this family volunteer to stay back with your young son, so if we need any help, you could help us?"

She watched her husband and without any consideration said, "Yes big brother Jacobus, I will only for you. Always and forever I will do as you all ask, for this is my family."

Our library was afterward converted into a hotel room. The library had twin beds brought into it where everyone would sleep and hopefully awaken as our dreams would break. I only wondered how would we all awaken if we are all placed to sleep by the spirits of Kasteel Vrederic? The windows were left open a little for fresh winter air to pour in. The open fireplace was turned on for enough heat. Soft sweet music was playing on Papa's gramophone as he wanted to travel in style.

Papa then asked the spirits, "We will all travel back together right? For I would like to see my son married off to his beloved in this life. For I too want to hold on to you my dear spirit of Kasteel Vrederic and say, 'Opa's heart beats your name' too."

I watched Griet come forward and say, "I only pray you all come back safely as this is not an easy journey. For even though you all might feel like you are just asleep here, you will feel all the pain and joy physically over there and here. So it is very important to remember you must have someone to bring you all back here."

Mama came to my side and said, "I have traveled through the tunnel of dreams without planning any of it. I just woke up the next morning realizing it was all a dream. Yet I understand as you hold on to the diary, she has her own powers and she will guide you to the pages she wants you to travel to. I hope the spirits of Kasteel Vrederic can guide us with all of the unanswered questions of our minds."

Griet and Theunis both watched us as Theunis said, "We will do whatever it takes to keep our future family members safe. For you all are our future lineage. Yet we want Jacobus to hold on to the book and only think of Rietje crying in the same library trying to figure out how she would keep this castle and her grandfather's beloved diaries safe. We will hold your hands one by one and then you will travel through a tunnel."

He watched his wife as she was tearing up in fear. I knew my child from whatever time period she might be, as she was scared like her mother. I knew on one hand, she was frightened for all of us if we were being placed at risk, but on the other hand, she was scared for her child who was fighting all on her own.

I told her, "Griet my child, all is well for if we don't travel, then we will be no more. However, by taking the risk and traveling time we all have a chance of being alive in the twenty-first century. So come on be a good girl and help this Papa of yours. For remember young woman, whatever time period you might be in, I am always and forever your Papa."

She watched me and wiped off her tears as she told all of us, "Okay my family, let's do this and again I shall have a chance to take a journey with my Papa, be it in spirit form."

Mama told everyone, "I want to warn all of you to be very careful as this traveling is similar to traveling through the tunnel of light and walking toward death. For in the tunnel of light, there are different doors one may take. We all must walk alone yet remember not to look backward. This tunnel is very risky for if we look backward, we will fall and may not return to the place we want to land at but land at a separate place. We must all walk toward the door of dreams, not the door of reincarnation."

Mama watched Papa and held on to him as she then said, "Please do not walk into any Ferris wheel as then you will be in the door of reincarnation. I will make sure while we are returning to place our beloved spirits of Kasteel Vrederic into the wagon of reincarnation. Yet I must take the route and make sure they land at the right place. I am positive Margriete has been reborn, yet I must make sure she lands here in our time period as an adult. Griet, my dear grandchild, you and your husband must leave a reflection of yourselves in the lighthouse while you travel with me. For I will take you up to the door of reincarnation on our trip back. From there you must travel on your own and find yourselves back home to us. I know it's hard but our prayers will bring both of you back home to us."

I watched the two lovebirds as they watched one another and I knew they were thinking what they should do. Being together for centuries I knew they were terrified of being separated for a few years. Yet they would be gifted another chance to raise their child themselves if only they both agree.

Theunis then said, "I would love to be back in flesh to only unite with you my beloved wife. Then we could raise our Rietje and be there with her and her beloved Opa. For I know this is the route we must take."

My spirit child only nodded as she went closer toward her grandmother and said, "I trust you my grandmother and yes I will do as you say for I shall never let you go. I would love to be with you and have a chance to know the great woman who kept and brought all the family members of Kasteel Vrederic together."

My mother then said, "I shall bring you back, and these are my vows from the beyond."

Then as the lights were dimmed and all were quiet, I watched the spirits of the castle touch the foreheads of all of us, one after another and everyone started to fall asleep. I realized as I was falling asleep, a small child's hands touched me. He said in a baby voice, "Big bro don't leave me again.

I don't like being separated from my family. I traveled alone before. Don't leave me alone."

Sleep was taking over my eyes as I tried to see my nephew who was crying and ran toward my mother. He then cried out to her and said, "Big Mama's heart beats Andries. Where Big Mama go, I go. Never separate from me ever again woman."

I watched him jump on top of Mama as Katelijne too tried to stop him but fell asleep on the carpet with her head on top of Mama's chest and her son on top of Mama's heart. I only heard Theunis say, "Oh no Jacobus here we go. No one is left behind to awaken any one of us as all the members of the twenty-first-century Kasteel Vrederic are on route to the seventeenth-century Kasteel Vrederic, traveling through the tunnel of dreams."

DREAMS

From across the ocean

Of timeless eternity,

I saw you,

My beloved granddaughter,

My majestical, beautiful granddaughter,

Who lives across the mystical ocean of life.

Yet I asked all,

How do I cross over to her land?

If I were the majestical phoenix,

Maybe I could attempt

To fly over

The unseen, unknown skies,

Yet today I found another way,

A magical door

Which I could open and then,

You would see me

And I could see you.

Even if it is for only a while,

Even for a day

Or maybe two,

This magical door

Would allow us to be together.

If only you believe,

My beloved granddaughter.

For this grandfather,

Now my child,

Close your eyes,

And then open your eyes to believe

In the magical door of,

DREAMS.

Dear Rietje,

Today I would like you to close your eyes and travel through the magical door I will open for you. For through this door I have traveled to you. Through this door I am able to see you, even though time and tide keep us separated. Yet if you only believe in this magical door then you too shall be able to travel time and tide and come and see me, whenever your heart so desires. So as you close your eyes tonight, why don't you open your eyes to the magical door of dreams? Believe in dreams and start to travel time and then you shall be with us whenever your heart so desires.

Love you eternally,

Opa

CHAPTER THREE:

Traveling Through The Tunnel Of Light

"The unanswered questions are those that have not been asked, so we must ask, seek, and knock for all the answers of life."

The Kasteel Vrederic family of the twenty-first century travels time to Kasteel Vrederic of the seventeenth century to help their ancestors.

I was walking through a tunnel where everything was made out of light. It looked like a whirlwind circling all around me. A tunnel was going under the cold sea, yet all the seawater was made out of light. The twirling tunnel never felt dizzy and never made me queasy. I had a happy feeling as if I was free from all the burdens of life. I wanted to keep on walking forward and knew I would meet my Creator soon. A magical feeling it was yet then I heard a scream from behind me. I tried to stop walking and look behind me to see who was screaming.

With all my energy gathered up, I looked back, yet in front of me I heard a voice say, "Dear child, if you look back you will travel back to life and remember life might not be a joyous ride. Yet if that is your will, then do look back, otherwise keep on walking forward."

I heard from behind me my mother was screaming and actually for the first time thought she was shouting at me. The small petite woman shouted at the top of her voice and kept on calling my name.

I heard her say, "Jacobus Vrederic van Phillip, don't you dare walk that way, for I told you to only walk into the dream tunnel. That's why not everyone can make this journey. Walking through the tunnel of light is not easy my son. Come and hold my hands and walk through the tunnel of dreams only."

I then somehow came to my senses and knew what I must do. I could not see my family members yet I kept on hearing my mother's voice call upon all of us. She was then screaming her lungs out as she said, "Antonius, Big Mama's heart beats your name. Come and hold me as I need you now. Don't walk away from me my child. Please come and hold my hands."

It was then I was able to see Papa walking toward the direction I was walking toward. I screamed and told my father, "Papa don't you dare leave me I tell you, for I need your strong shoulders to lean on right now. Papa I love you and I really am blessed to have you. Please Papa help."

I heard and saw Papa come near me and say, "I am not going anywhere, leaving you or the petite woman who holds my heart. Here hold my hands and let's find our family together."

I saw my mother and father stand next to me as then I watched my brother Antonius come near Mama and say, "Big Mama's heart beats Antonius." Before Mama could say anything, we all saw a young child run toward Mama and say, "No Big Mama's heart beats my name."

Mama held on to all of her three boys as she cried and smiled at the same time. She kissed Papa and said, "Don't you dare walk ahead of me, for I can't live life without you even for a day."

She watched all of us and said, "How did Andries come here if his mother is missing? Where is she? I know she fell asleep on top of me."

I knew something was wrong as I realized Katelijne had traveled through this tunnel before when she was pronounced dead and brought back to life. I only hoped she was able to walk again only toward the door of dreams.

I wondered what about Theunis and Griet? Where were they? I watched Mama and Papa and knew they were thinking of the same thing. My brother Antonius called for his wife with his shouting voice.

He said, "Sweetheart, I hope you are not sleeping again while I walk through the tunnel alone sleepless."

It was then we heard a soft and fragile voice say, "Antonius, help. I am scared as I had done this before. I am worried if I will be able to walk through this without falling again."

It was then my mother who said, "Andries, what is wrong with you? Baby boy are you okay?"

We all saw a mother Katelijne run through the tunnel to her child. She touched her baby boy and cried out in fear as she said, "My baby what is wrong with you? Are you all right? Mama is here."

Our little baby Andries said, "Woman you are Katelijne and Big Mama is my mother. Why do you keep on forgetting? I am your friend okay, but you are woman and Big Mama is my Mama."

Katelijne watched everyone as Mama said, "It matters not what he calls you sweetheart as you know he is your baby boy too. A mother's heart forgets all her troubles when her child needs her."

Katelijne said, "Antonius, our baby boy is a genius from a very young age. He talks and walks and now he has started to talk fluently. I think it's because he has walked through this tunnel twice now and because he remembers all of his past life stories."

It was then we saw Theunis and Griet too come closer to us. They were both tired and a little different as they were more physical and more visible than before.

Theunis asked Mama, "You are our guide until we get out of here. Yet I would want to know why does it feel different in here?"

Mama watched me and I told her it's okay say what you must, all with a nod of my head. I knew my mother knew my mind even without uttering any words.

Mama watched everyone as she said, "You two had missed walking into the tunnel before so in order to take us back in time, you have walked into the tunnel of light. Now after we return, you two must walk through the reincarnation tunnel. It's your destiny. I will tie a ribbon on your hands so as you walk upon the Ferris wheel, you two will land upon the same place. You will be reborn to only reunite with one another all over again. Remember it will feel like a minute or so to you both when we meet again even though it will be years for us. I promise Griet, you will be reborn to your blessed father all over again."

Theunis asked Mama, "Grandmother-in-law, please tell me I will find Griet, my beloved, all over again. For where shall I be reborn from?"

Mama watched him and said, "You two will have an easy reunion as you two died at the same place and I believe you two will find one another much more easily than all of the others. For we were all separated in death and had to find one another by calling one another through our heartbeats. I called upon my twin flame through the door of dreams. Katelijne called her twin flame through the sound of heartbeats. Margriete and Jacobus shall have to fight their own battle and call upon one another as you two must call upon one another again. You shall for I shall wait for all of you to find one another, these are my vows from the beyond."

We all heard cries and screams from somewhere ripping the Earth, the seas, and the skies. These cries were from a person who was very dear to our hearts. Yet we stood in the tunnel trying to figure out which door was the door of dreams. We walked in fear of getting lost and turning into the wrong door.

The tunnel was lighted and very big yet it was very confusing. We tried to stay together and had tied a rope on to one another as we did not want to be separated at any cost. I saw strangers walk obliviously through the tunnel not knowing who we were or who they were. It seemed like everyone just knew where they had to go. It was hard for a doctor to watch people walking through this tunnel I had heard so many patients talk about. It gave me the shivers yet in a different kind of way. I realized it was not that bad. For it's the route everyone must take. Here everyone was walking through it so bravely, and as if so peacefully.

My father watched me and as a painter himself said, "It's amazing as I can see myself and Antonius create an amazing portrait of life and its true ending yet the beginning too. We would call this the amazing tunnel of light. Yet I know what a doctor like you are thinking. You are wondering if you could have been there for the young ones and had given them another chance at life. However, do you realize this is a second chance at life? Everything that ends, begins again."

I saw the depth of a painter's thoughts and felt much better and asked everyone, "How do we get out of here and end at the seventeenth-century Kasteel Vrederic?"

Mama watched all of us and said, "It's easy. Follow the callings of our guide. She will take us to her, just have faith. For remember all you have to say is, 'Dear entranced beloved, I shall never let you go.'"

We all said nothing yet I knew everyone was calling our beloved Rietje and knew she would give us a signal. The diary started to glow as we all saw again in the diary, a letter appeared from the seventeenth-century Rietje.

The letter appeared in front of us as we all wanted to read it at the same time. So I read it out loud to my family.

Dear Opa,

I am a little confused as strange writings and words are appearing in my diary. Sir Alexander has said the diary must be haunted, yet I know somehow it's your handwriting. I told him the diary is magical. I believe my Opa is trying to communicate with us from the beyond. I only hope since your words are appearing on the pages of the diary, may my words too land within your blessed hands.

I wonder if the stories you have written are true and you are arriving from the future. Right now I know you are stuck in some kind of a tunnel. I will keep on singing my song that Mama had sung to me as a child. I hope you will hear my song "Through Your Mama's Eyes" and I hope this will guide you toward us.

You had taught me to ask, seek, and knock when in need of help. So I will keep on asking where are you Opa, and I will knock on my wall as to give you my direction, and I will seek you as I keep on writing to you within my blessed diary.

Also Opa, you are not moving here and Oma too has fallen asleep on top of your chest. She keeps on repeating how could your heart not beat if her heart still beats? She said she only waits for that time when you will come and bury her yourself. For she refuses to accept you are no more. She told all of us to watch and see how you will come and bury her yourself. I have brushed her hair and kept her tidy as she said you would be upset when you see her untidy and in pain. Opa, everyone had told me I look just like Oma, brown hair and fair skin, yet today my Oma has gray streaks and very pale skin from loss of blood. I wish I knew how I could have done something different to save my Opa and very weak and tired Oma, who refuses to see her own suffering.

She believes your love for her and her love for you will break even Heaven and Earth as you will appear. Opa, she keeps on saying, "You will all be ashamed of yourselves as in front of your eyes, my Jacobus will come and bury me with his kisses. For how could he die if I am still alive? Also how could I go on living if he is no more?"

I have kept both of you, myself, and Sir Alexander, who too is wounded yet breathing, hidden in your secret room behind the library shelves. Oma calls this room "Jacobus's safe room."

Also Opa, could you hurry please as I really need your help. Yet Opa don't worry as I am your brave little girl.

I am your little Rietje.

P.S. Please remember, "Opa's heart beats Rietje."

After I read the letter out loud to my family, I just started to walk. We all followed the sounds of the amazing musical voice of an amazing young woman. We knew her knocking, seeking, and asking took us to an amazing door which read "Seventeenth-Century Kasteel Vrederic." We realized then our faith and belief finally led us to our destination by traveling through the tunnel of light.

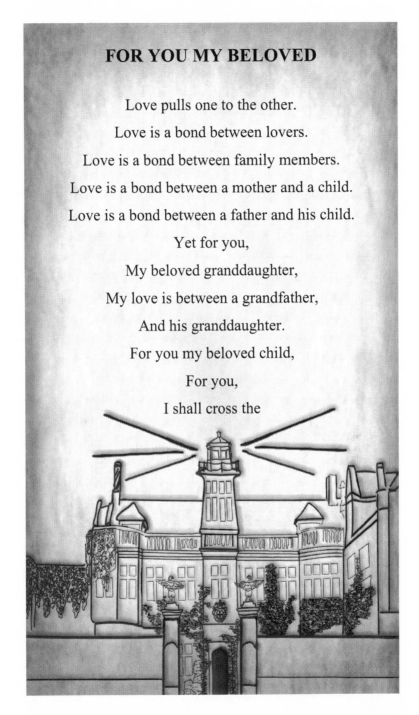

FOR YOU MY BELOVED

Love pulls one to the other.

Love is a bond between lovers.

Love is a bond between family members.

Love is a bond between a mother and a child.

Love is a bond between a father and his child.

Yet for you,

My beloved granddaughter,

My love is between a grandfather,

And his granddaughter.

For you my beloved child,

For you,

I shall cross the

Blue ocean,

The ever-blue skies,

The green fields.

For you dear entranced beloved granddaughter,

This grandfather

Will even cross time.

For you my dear,

I have now entered the tunnel of light,

Only and forever,

FOR YOU MY BELOVED.

Dear Rietje,

Today we have entered the tunnel of light to be only with you. I wanted you to know this Opa of yours shall always be with you physically if possible. However, if not physically possible, then I shall be with you spiritually forever and eternally.

Remember my dear child, this Opa's heart always and forever beats your name. I hope and pray, we can meet through a magical door eternally. I will answer your magical calls from the beyond, even though we don't have any connections we can magically call one another through.

In my time period, we have a connection we can call one another through which is known as a phone call. This will be invented much later than your time period. The telephone will arrive in 1876. Yet it still won't connect between time centuries. Here we also can see one another through our phone calls, which makes keeping in touch so much easier. I asked my Mama, your Great-Oma if we could have had a way to keep in touch in between centuries. She told me actually if you believe, we can through the door of blessed dreams.

So we must keep our connection to one another through the magical door of love and dreams. For when you miss me, just close your eyes, and I shall be there to kiss you on your head as I had placed you to bed as a tiny baby. You were a very arrogant child and had wanted this Opa to always kiss you good night every night. I know even now this grandfather shall blow a kiss across the centuries and you shall be able to catch all my blessings and kisses through your blessed dreams. Remember all you have to do is believe. Also Rietje yes, Opa's heart beats Rietje.

Love you infinitely,

Opa

CHAPTER FOUR:

The Seventeenth-Century Kasteel Vrederic

"All is same as you had left, yet when you open your eyes after closing them for a while, you realize you are standing exactly where you were, however, you have just traveled time."

Erasmus van Phillip plays with his adopted son's reincarnated form, now his grandson, Andries van Phillip.

T he twirling lights of the tunnel dimmed suddenly. Then I saw darkness evolve all around us. I heard the birds singing and felt the morning dew under my feet. I could smell fresh wildflowers blooming around us. Near my feet laid forget-me-nots, I had planted with my granddaughter Rietje. Her tiny fingers would plant each flower gently and then come and kiss my cheeks after each one she had planted.

The little pattering sounds of her feet would awaken all the members of Kasteel Vrederic. I knew I was dreaming again. For it felt like I was back in the seventeenth-century garden behind my library. The same garden I watched over from my secret veiled corner of the library.

It was the thought of my concealed library door and my lifetime during the seventeenth century that jolted me back to reality. I stood up and realized we were standing in a spot that today is the sitting room of the library. I searched for my family members as I saw they were all sleeping in the same spot they all fell asleep in. Yet there were no sofas or tables. There were no walls or a room either as the room attached to the library did not exist in the seventeenth century.

I realized it was added on as renovations were done by our ancestors throughout the years. The castle too changed her colors as the inhabitants changed. I saw Papa was sleeping peacefully on the grass as Mama was sleeping next to him. I was shocked to see Andries sleeping on top of Mama. Katelijne too was wide awake trying to wake up her husband, my brother Antonius.

He woke up saying, "I don't think I slept well. I feel groggy and tired. I will wake up Katelijne in a minute and make breakfast for the family today. I remember it's my day to make breakfast."

I went to Mama and Papa as I watched them awaken by themselves. Mama was fast as she knew immediately where she was.

She said, "Jacobus we did not take to plan where the hidden closet in the room was. This part must have been added on. We are all standing in open air. Okay everyone let's get up and rescue our baby Rietje. By the way Jacobus where is the war and the horses and warriors or the army? I don't see anyone."

I knew what Mama was saying. Everything looked so quiet as if the Earth was at a standstill and we were all transported to a place before the addition to the library. I asked my father, "Did you add on the library sitting room or did grandmother do it before you?"

He replied and said, "No I did not, and your grandmother could not have as they had lost Kasteel Vrederic when they defaulted on their mortgage. I bought it back from the bank and did do renovations to make it look historical. Yet I don't know who added on. I tried to look into it but the castle was vacant for a long time. No one bought it as all thought it was haunted."

My brother Antonius started to laugh loudly as he said, "Haunted by our family I am presuming. I believe if anyone other than our family had bought the castle they too would run in fear of the hauntings. We are a very scary bunch."

We all watched baby Andries cry as he then went to his mother not Big Mama and said, "Now woman, carry me up now! Andries scared of ghosts."

Big Mama laughed aloud and said, "Woman carry my baby boy and don't drop him in fear of the ghosts when you see one."

Katelijne really got scared and said, "Everyone, are we lost or what is going on? I am now worried I never said my farewell to my father. What if he starts to wonder why we all went missing?"

Antonius watched his wife and they both laughed at the same time. Katelijne told us, "It's going to be all right as

Papa knows if we do go missing, we will be lost in the castle as he believes this is a magical place where even the Lover's Lighthouse shall guide everyone when it is necessary."

I then saw behind all of us was standing a very realistic looking couple, the lovers of the lighthouse. I saw for the first time my daughter Griet standing in front of me. She surprisingly looked like Mama but somehow a lot like me too. Her magical black hair glowed in the early dawn's sunlight. Her olive-colored skin told everyone she was a majestical princess.

Then I watched Theunis, a six-foot-tall, very muscular warrior standing in front of us. His majestical blond hair stood beyond his shoulders and sparkled like magic. His magical blue eyes stared at his wife which retold a story of love only the eternally beloveds would have for one another throughout time.

I walked toward both and gave them a hug. I kissed my daughter and told her, "I do have you now and I promise my child, until I have you again as my own, I shall never let you go."

I watched my father walk toward her as he watched her with so much emotion and said, "Dear child, this Opa promises you from here on my heart beats your name too. For I too shall not rest until I have your mother and you back in my heart physically. Now let's go and rescue my great-granddaughter and her chosen groom and all whom we can save."

I knew what he meant by that as I too lived in fear of what I would find myself in and how would my iron-clad heart be able to take all of it and just keep my buried love and loss just buried in there. I watched the castle where I had first met Margriete. The carriage house was standing in front of us where we had first made love. In the twenty-first century, however, we have a huge guest house standing in its place.

In the twenty-first century, no horses or wagons shared the same quarters we had united as a couple within. The memories were alive as if it happened days ago. I know the love of my life was in there fighting for her life, as she laid on top of the love of her life. It was strange as I knew it was my own self yet I felt strange and somewhat I wondered if I felt jealous of my own dead self.

My parents were watching me and I knew both of them very well knew my inner feelings. I knew I wouldn't show any of my feelings if I could control them. However all my feelings would be written for my precious granddaughter to read.

My father watched me and said, "My son I know how you feel and what you are going through. Because even if they are your cuts, I somehow bleed from them."

I watched my brother watch both of us as he asked, "Okay everyone, where is Andries? Big Mama did you see him?"

We all then watched a runaway toddler running toward his home as he screamed, "Andries wants to go home and Andries wants his pillow and his big bear and his sippy cup."

We all felt good he was talking much more in complete sentences even though he calls himself by his given name. The boy wanted to go home and knew his house even in the seventeenth century. Yet we all knew this could be dangerous if he landed in the wrong hands. I watched my nephew run faster than any one of us and walk into the enemy camp, that once was our home.

We all ran after the little toddler and landed into our home which was inundated by the Spaniards and felt like an enemy camp, not our home. The home was not empty but all the goons were asleep as it was early dawn. I watched my small mother walk bravely toward the library as if no one saw her. She stopped in front of a man with swords and placed her tongue out and even made a sound. I was terrified for her and saw no one even moved at her gesture.

Then my brother Antonius went after her and said, "Big Mama, it's my turn. May I?"

Then he did the same gesture and I watched Andries come flying into Mama's hands and asked, "Big Mama, it's my turn now?"

Then Papa walked toward Mama and lifted her in his arms and said, "My brave wife, you know very well they can't see or hear you. So you are walking ahead of everyone. Yet I remember not so long ago, you screamed and told me to hide you in my chest."

She watched Papa and said, "Forever keep me in your chest Erasmus."

I heard Katelijne and Antonius say, "Oh Big Mama and Big Papa making out through words."

Then out of nowhere, spine-shivering, thrilling, tear-jerking cries of a woman whose voice sounded so familiar yet so different broke the air. I tried to jerk back my memories. My mother grabbed my shirt and stopped me on spot as she said, "Jacobus remember you cannot have Margriete see you for then she will lose her mind as she needs to grieve and let destiny take over. She was yours and will be yours in this life if you only believe and let fate be.

We are here to only change Rietje's fate so that you and Margriete and all of the future generations have a chance. We can't change the fate of all others, including Margriete's. For then you won't see her in the future and if you don't exist, then Mama and Papa too won't unite. You do understand my son, you must be strong."

I could not answer as my brother Antonius answered for me and said, "He might be the medical doctor on board but I am his brother who is here to make sure we finish the job and go back home safely. All of us together, just like we came, we shall all return together. Even if it means I have to take my big brother over my shoulders and carry him home through the tunnel of light, I will."

I knew my family members were all worried about me. I promised to myself I wouldn't be selfish. I wouldn't sacrifice my love for my love. I would keep myself chained within the controlled cold showers so I don't ruin my family and my evermore beloved Margriete. For you my darling, I will keep myself away from you. For the other women in my life, my mother, my daughter and my granddaughter I too will chain myself and be emotionless.

I only told everyone, "I will be all right, for I know when I fall, Papa will hold on to me. If I slip, my brother will help me stay steady. Yet if I need a soft corner, I have my mother and my sister to hide away into."

It was so strange as no one said anything yet in the silence I found my strength as I knew we would always be there for one another, even throughout time. I got steady on my feet and hoped I would not fall off track at the sight of Margriete and Rietje.

The cold winter winds blew in fallen leaves into the unkept courtyard of Kasteel Vrederic. My home, our pride, our castle was in the ruins. I felt anger brew within my inner soul as I watched all of this.

Papa watched all of this and was numb for a while as he held on to my hands and Antonius's and said, "A doctor must keep his patience at all times, for you never know when you are about to perform a surgery. A painter must keep his temper under control, for only then would he be able to create a masterpiece. Also Anadhi and Katelijne remember a mother too must be calm and not become wild as she must first take care of her children."

My mother watched my father and said, "Yes my dear I understand and agree with you, yet remember a woman becomes a mother for her child as she can become a snake if her child is at risk. Yet for you my husband I will carefully choose my role, I promise."

We all followed the sounds of the cries and came upon a room where everything went silent. I wondered where Theunis and Griet were, as they had been missing for a while. I realized they were in spirit form and still were so they knew they could walk about freely. Yet we did not realize we too were there in spirit form. That was why we could see them so clearly, not because they became more humanlike but instead we became more like spirits. It felt strange to be able to see and hear everything yet not communicate with everyone.

We rushed toward the sounds and realized the sounds were not heard by normal humans as they were hidden within stone walls. Yet we could hear them clearly because of our condition. It was then I walked into my library of the seventeenth century and realized it felt like I had never left.

My family followed me to a door where I knew exactly how to push open a bookcase and enter a safe room which was hidden from the world. The room in itself was very small and dark. No candles were there but somehow a lantern was lit in the corner. There were rags left on the floor which were red, covered in blood. There was a bucket of water and I saw in the corner was a basket filled with bread and fresh churned butter. I watched they used chamber pots as toilets and someone was keeping up the cleaning and refilling fresh water and rags.

There in my hands I saw the diary of my precious Rietje glow like magic, as did a diary in the corner of the room. I watched a very elegant woman with long brown hair and fair skin walk toward the diary. I knew she looked so much like Margriete yet she was different. In front of me there stood my entranced beloved granddaughter Rietje.

I wrote in my diary,

"Dear Entranced Beloved Granddaughter,

I am standing in front of you. For you, somehow I have crossed time and now am here as I will walk with you throughout your darkest days."

I watched my little Rietje, one of the beholders of my heartbeats, write back with her quill pen,

"Opa,

Please at least one more time do say, 'Opa's heart beats Rietje'. Also Opa welcome back to the seventeenth-century Kasteel Vrederic."

OPEN YOUR EYES

My beloved grandchild,
Close your eyes and see me,
As then you can imagine me
Just the way
I had left you.
For in that time and that hour,
We were both
So close to one another.
For a grandfather
Always loves his grandchild.
Even though time passes by,

The love and bond stay still

For love is not material.

Like water,

It does not flow away,

Nor like the wind,

Does it blow away.

It does not

Even follow the storms

Of life that come and go.

For my love for you

And your love for me,

Travels invisibly

From my soul

To yours.

Open your eyes

My beloved granddaughter,

And now forever

Keep your memories of me

Stored safely within your inner chest.

For I will hold on to

Your memories safely tucked away

Within my chest,

Near my own heartbeats.

Remember my dear,

You too keep my memories

Near your heartbeats.

For even if one of our hearts still beats,

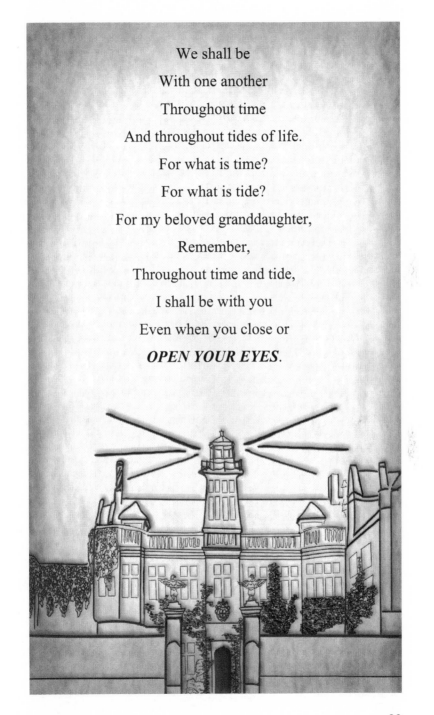

We shall be

With one another

Throughout time

And throughout tides of life.

For what is time?

For what is tide?

For my beloved granddaughter,

Remember,

Throughout time and tide,

I shall be with you

Even when you close or

OPEN YOUR EYES.

Dear Rietje,

Today I would want you to open your eyes to the door of time traveling. It's an amazing subject not thought about by the normal human minds. Yet there are some people who believe in the door of reincarnation. As through this door, people travel time after death to be with their beloved family members and their twin flames even beyond one life.

Yet in our family, we also believe in the door of dreams as we travel to one another through this magical door we call dreams. For through this door, I am able to travel to your time period as you too can travel to my time period. So I would ask you to give this magical door a chance as I will see you soon through this magical door of dreams. I love you endlessly my beloved granddaughter.

Yours truly,

Opa

CHAPTER FIVE:

Margriete, Evermore Beloved, I Shall Never Let You Go

"Time and tide wash everything as they pass by yet love remains intact eternally within the hearts of the evermore beloveds."

Twenty-first-century Dr. Jacobus Vrederic van Phillip travels time with his family and is confronted with his own dying form being hovered over by his Margriete van Wijck and Margriete "Rietje" Jacobus Peters in the seventeenth century.

S orrow and grief filled up the small, hidden, stone-walled safe room. A very small room I had built during the Dutch Eighty Years' War. A war I knew was finally over, and the Netherlands found her victory on May 15th, 1648. Yet today as my family and I had traveled back in time, we had landed within the war my family and I had fought and died in years ago. It somehow felt strange to walk into a time period where I knew I too had fought till my last breath. I had lost my son-in-law Theunis Peters and my only daughter Griet van Jacobus to this war.

Within this war, I had fought another war which was brewing all around Europe and America and worldwide, called the unjust witch burnings. As a nobleman, I had tried to save not only the women in my family but men and women all across my country from the unjust witch hunts. Through the door of reincarnation, I finally found my parents in the twenty-first century to only travel back in time through the door of dreams to the seventeenth-century, war-ravaged land to again fight for my family.

I am thankful I was allowed to be able to do this, miraculously, yet I only wish I could have done more. I watched a small fragile woman who had aged gracefully sleeping on top of a man who looked so much like myself yet much older. No smell of death crowded the walled-in room yet I knew death was suspended all over here like a dark haze. I heard sobs coming very slightly from a fragile old woman recurrently. All my courage left my inner soul as I felt I had no ground beneath my feet. An empty feeling evolved all around my inner self and I knew all the war and struggles I had crossed throughout reincarnation and rebirth, this was my harshest war. I must control all my temptations and urge to comfort my twin flame from mourning my own death.

How could I tell you I have moved on through the tunnel of light into another time period, only waiting for you? I know you too have moved on, for how could you not move on if I have moved on? You know we have two separate bodies yet one love and one flame. I burn for you and my flame is quenched only by you.

Antonius came and stood next to me and said, "Think of something else. Remember what you had said, 'Death does not prevent you from loving someone.' Let her mourn and let go of the pain as she will awaken in her own time. You must keep the memories alive and wait to recreate new ones with her as you cross the border of time again."

I watched my younger brother watch me with so much love. I knew I would be all right as I had his shoulders to lay all my troubles upon.

My nephew, my brother reincarnated, could barely talk yet started to speak like a bird. He came over and said, "Big bro, it's going to be all right. I have your back."

I realized somehow Andries was in there, Antonius's twin, my younger brother was inside of my nephew and tried to express his feelings, yet age got in the way. But we all understood what he was trying to say.

Papa took him on his lap and said, "I won't lose any one of my sons as it's too much to handle. I lost Andries and that was too much. I never realized how I would have dealt with the loss of my son Jacobus van Vrederic as I had my son's reincarnated form Jacobus Vrederic van Phillip with me. Yet today my Creator has sent me back in time to see how I, a father, who had passed away before his son would deal with his death in front of my eyes."

Then we all saw my mother as she was sitting in the corner crying for a son she had given birth to but could never have. A son she cried for and brought back to her through the blessed door of reincarnation, yet now she was watching him pass away again. It was the memories of Jacobus van Vrederic that had led her to Papa. My mother recently had gone through another period of sadness with the loss of Andries, as she had made his gravesite her second home until he too came back as my nephew. I know how broken up she was until I was reborn again. It was then I realized what had I done? I was so immersed in my own pain I forgot my parents and their inner feelings.

I walked over to my mother and asked her, "Mama does it help at all as I am standing right here next to you?"

Mama watched me and said, "Does it help at all that you know she is waiting for you on the other side of the world in the twenty-first century? You must find her and then bring your daughter and granddaughter back through the door of reincarnation, if you only believe."

I realized my mother was not only suffering but also trying to make sure I realize where my footing should be in this situation. I hugged her and kissed her head and told her, "Mama I know where my heart is, for I know 'Mama's heart beats Jacobus' yet I can't control my feelings for the granddaughter I had raised with my own hands. It is only for her I am here and after I reunite her with Sir Alexander and get rid of the enemies of Kasteel Vrederic, I will peacefully return back home, from the *I Shall Never Let You Go* time period to the *Vows From The Beyond* time period."

We all got up as we saw the young woman with long brown hair and petite build walk across from us to her grandmother.

She said, "Oma please don't leave me alone. I am scared to be alone without Opa. All my life I only had Opa and you. At least now do tell me how I survive in this war without you two. Please be strong like he was when you were missing. I will be strong like Opa and I will fight all by myself. I told Opa I would become a warrior and go join the resistance army. Yet Opa said I can fight here and find a suitor for myself at home. He told me my suitor would come to me. He did get wounded, however. How did he know I would be fighting a war at home?"

She then watched toward us as if she could see someone and shook her head as she again watched toward our direction. I then saw Griet and Theunis stand in the corner of the room.

Rietje watched her parents and said, "Mama, Papa, are they here? Can they see me or hear me? Why is it I can see you two but not them?"

She then said, "Opa are you here? You promised I would never be alone and you would be with me always. Please help me. You taught me everything, how to be a proper lady, how to be an educated woman, and a warrior, yet you never taught me how to live my life without you."

I heard Katelijne and Mama cry as did Griet at the words of Rietje. My father and brother just stood near Theunis, as if they were waiting for the brave warrior to take control of the war-ravaged Kasteel Vrederic.

Theunis watched everyone as he watched his own daughter, and I knew the father inside of his soul needed a break. It was then I watched my baby nephew walk over to him and very plainly say, "I am tired. Can you lift me up please? I now want to sleep. Now sing a lullaby and put me to sleep."

The boy just jumped up into the comforting hands of the male spirit of Kasteel Vrederic. I watched a warrior who had only known how to fight in a war become the comforting hands of a man. I wondered who was comforting whom, as I knew my brother Andries who had been the pianist who always played sweet musical notes to comfort all souls was still in him. It was then I saw a warrior walk in through the stone wall into the small safe room.

He rushed in with fresh towels and water as he said, "Rietje, how is Oma? Has her fever reduced? Is Opa breathing or has he stopped breathing? For I can't tell if he is still with us or not. His breathing is so slow I feel like he has passed away, yet his body is fighting for someone or something. We are getting more soldiers from the enemy camp as they are all trying to say the castle is not haunted and they want Kasteel Vrederic to be their war site. They are going to make this home their official grounds. I am sorry Rietje as I tried to keep my given promise to your grandfather, that I would keep you and Kasteel Vrederic safe and secure until we can pass this on to our next generation."

We then saw our Rietje walk over to Sir Alexander and punch him in his chest. A small petite woman just took over a huge knight clad in a knight's attire. I watched Antonius scream and say, "That's my grandniece! Way to go girl! Show him you are of the bloodline of a true Vrederic."

Katelijne watched her husband and said, "Antonius be quiet! He is injured."

It was then I saw Rietje say to him, "Are you hurt? I am sorry. I wanted to remind you I had taken an oath if Opa does not walk me through the aisle, I will remain a maiden and never marry. I won't break my vows for anyone. So no future generations from me at least."

Sir Alexander van der Bijl then laughed and said, "In this life sweetheart, then you will remain a maiden, and even I won't marry if I can't have you. Yet my entranced beloved,

I shall never let you go, in this life or any other. That's my oath brave one."

The whole room was filled in joy and happiness as my mother got up and said, "He passed my test. He said the words entranced beloved, I shall never let you go, without even traveling to the future. He knew they would have a life together as entranced lovers and husband and wife. We have to get to work family. He will marry my great-granddaughter. I have to plan a wedding before I leave."

I watched my mother, Katelijne, and Griet start to plan a wedding while Papa, Antonius, Theunis with a baby boy in his arms, and I were all worried how to free our home from the enemies.

I watched Margriete get up and walk to Rietje who was still crying. Margriete looked pale and undernourished. She looked like she had some kind of fever brewing in her. I wondered if she was hurt and never showed Rietje, as that would be her character. She walked funny and I saw her feet had blood dripping from them. She was shot in the foot somehow and it seemed infected. I hoped not gangrene.

It was then Rietje said, "Oma don't walk. Your foot is hurt. You got shot as you tried to fight the goons for shooting Opa. How could you jump in front of shooting bullets Oma? Why would you? You got multiple bullets in your body. I need to take you to a doctor and get you healed."

Margriete kissed Rietje and said, "Sweetheart, my dear child, how could I keep on breathing if the beholder of my breath stops breathing? I told him it's my heartbeat that beats in his heart. I must join my love and my life soon, for I know he won't be able to walk through the door of death without me."

She held steady for a while as if trying to keep her strength for her love for her granddaughter.

Then she said, "He is gone yet he awaits my arrival. The promises were made. My eyes, his tears, and his eyes, my tears. So you see with his lifeless body, I can't even cry, as he stole all my tears. However, my heart only screams and shouts for him. The water of love that pours from my eyes has dried up. I must go to him, but I must make sure our beloved granddaughter is happily married off to her beloved. I don't have much time my dear yet I want you to have a blessed life filled with love and joy with your beloved."

She watched the lifeless body of Jacobus van Vrederic and ran toward him as she said, "My love, don't be scared. I will ask the sun to heat you and the stars to keep the showers of starry nights lit for you. Remember my love in life or in death, I shall never let you go. I will follow you throughout the dark nights and the sunny mornings throughout time."

She fainted on top of him. I knew she was dying from bullet wounds she took for her husband as I would find out how this all took place. Yet my whole interior just ripped open into pieces as I too knew the promises we had made. It was strange how I knew and remembered all of our promises.

I went over to the wall and realized I could walk outside and scream my heart out as I told my Creator, "We are both one soul with two bodies. If I have crossed over and awakened, then why has she not? How do I live when I know she is fighting death?"

Antonius followed me out as he said, "I had thought life is about living not dying. So even though death comes to one, the other one lives for both as they promised to live with each other, they live for one another."

I watched my brave brother who had fallen in love with a woman knowing she was dead. Yet his faith in love brought her back to him. I realized I too shall bury all my love and all my desires for you Margriete. I only hope as today we are separated by time, may tomorrow we be united at the same time.

Today I will kiss you from afar in my mind as I know tomorrow I will have you in my arms and kiss you physically as you are the only one I had, have, and shall always love. My dear Margriete, evermore beloved, I shall never let you go.

LOVE NEVER DIES

Love is found
From within.
Love only grows
From inward to outward.
No, you can't touch it,
Yet you can feel it.
You can't hear it,
Unless you hear
The breathing of
The one you love.
Yet even when the heartbeats
Of the one you love

Are no more,

Even then,

Your heart does not stop beating

For your one true beloved,

For it is true,

Even when your heart beats,

Or your beloved's heart beats no more,

Love lives on eternally and evermore as dear,

All lovers know this today and forever,

LOVE NEVER DIES.

My Dear Granddaughter,

Remember to hold on to your beloved, in life and even in death. For what is death? Is it not only that the physical body is no more? Keep faith alive as within our family we have lost a lot of lives. Yet with faith we learn to move on. It is never easy yet somehow I realized with or without the loved one, dawn still shines upon the skies. The glorious moon too comes and shines. Yet belief in twin flames and soul families keeps our family moving on.

Physically or spiritually, true twin flames become one when they unite once and for all. It is then they become one soul yet with two different bodies. The day I found and met your Oma, I realized I had found my true twin flame, my other half. I knew from us, our family would grow. From my twin flame, we created our soul family. Throughout centuries, our soul family keeps on growing.

Without her, I did not even want to be an individual, so how could I love any other human in this world? Yet as I found you my granddaughter, I knew you too were a gift from my beloved Margriete, and my daughter, my beloved Griet. So it was through you, I got back my Margriete and my lost daughter as it was then my love lived on.

So eternally, love lives on even after the death of the physical body. You too will see how through your children and grandchildren, we shall all live on eternally. You will always have all of us through your future generations. Today you know your future generations, your soul family lives on because you too had found your true twin flame. Remember my dear granddaughter, that's how love never dies.

Love always,

Opa

CHAPTER SIX:

Besieged Kasteel Vrederic

"Forcefully taking over a home through blood and battle will face its challenge as the bloodlines of the home's family members arrive riding the wagon of karma."

Dr. Jacobus Vrederic van Phillip stands with Sir Alexander van der Bijl and Margriete "Rietje" Jacobus Peters as they plan a way to take their home back from the Spanish army.

arely do I ever have emotional outbursts or show my emotions to anyone. Yet here I was all emotional and I worried if I could control my feelings. For here I was confronted by the very woman I became emotional or had perfected my control for. Yet today I watched the woman I gave my entire being to slide away from life in front of my eyes. I knew I had to get back on my feet and hold on to all that had given me the courage to be myself again.

I watched Theunis watch me and said, "I know you better than anyone in your current or previous lives. I have the advantage of watching my father-in-law like a friend over the centuries. Remember you got back up on your feet for your granddaughter. You had lost the love of your life but had the only ties with her left through your granddaughter. The one and only sign of your love lived with you through Rietje who reminded you every day of Margriete's words as she said, 'Opa's heart beats Rietje.' I want you to get up and fight for Rietje as she is the one who needs you. She is the one who needs to live on and have a life, not the one who had lived her life with her twin flame and so now wants to follow him through even death."

I watched my best friend, my son-in-law, and knew my warrior was back here once more to take us through another war zone. This time the war ground was our own home as our home had been besieged by the enemies. We might be the only inhabitants in history who had to fight for our own home from our home. Yet was it not said, home is where one feels the safest? I did wonder why we did not hear much of the soldiers outside. Maybe they were just here to have sex with the captured women so they were not looking to fight anyone.

I watched Rietje and knew she was not safe. She was terrified and wounded as she was a prisoner in her own home. I knew I must do what a doctor can do first. Save lives that could be saved. I called my family members.

I said, "Everyone, Theunis has something he would like to say, as we are all in his territory. He is and shall always be my noble warrior whom I had the pleasure to have worked with before."

As I watched Theunis, without uttering any words, I signaled him to proceed.

Theunis said, "I know we don't have much time as we can only be here for a while. You all need to work quickly and be back in your time period or you will be imprisoned here. So let's first get our doctor to heal all he can heal somehow. Then we must go out and get an account of all of our enemies. Observe them and plan and do as we must.

Don't wish to show yourselves to anyone, even by mistake. For you have an advantage of being invisible and have a disadvantage by showing yourselves to anyone who would want to trap you in this time period."

I watched Mama as she was quiet and said nothing. Yet I knew she knew even more than Theunis knew as she had traveled before through her dreams. Theunis was traveling through death. I watched my mother and knew she was going to say something she was not very happy to share but would say it anyway as I knew my mother.

Mama watched Theunis and said, "There is one difference between us as we are dream travelers. We can't control our journey if we divide and don't have the emotional control. By willing to show ourselves, we could show ourselves but even then we can't guarantee everyone would see us or not see us. For if we are related to them by the bond of knowing them in the past or in the future, then they will see us clearly. The bond could even be through marriage, such as Katelijne is married to Antonius who is from the same bloodline of Rietje. So she can and shall be able to participate by will. Yet she must be careful as I must as we were never here in this home before in our previous lives."

Mama watched everyone and then said, "We both come from the future. If we get lost in here, we won't be able to return to our time period but will be lost in oblivion forever and shall walk through the door of death. So we must stick with our husbands. Also remember we must awaken by a certain period, otherwise it will feel like sleep paralysis, which Jacobus can tell you is not dangerous but can be in some instances. In this instance, traveling through dreams can be dangerous. So we must all wake up quickly. Also someone must touch us to awaken us if we all get in the sleep paralysis situation. Also Jacobus must be careful not to stay behind or follow Margriete to another period as she has been reborn. Right now, we are time travelers traveling time through the dream tunnel to change some things in the past, not to be stuck here. So if you follow her, you too will be in the oblivion tunnel. Again Jacobus, you must go back to your time period to unite with Margriete."

Antonius said, "I will make sure I take my brother and my baby son back home with me. I will not risk anyone as well as my twin flame Katelijne. Big Papa hold on to Big Mama please because we can't risk her."

I watched my baby nephew who seemed like he understood everything that was being said. He had uttered to his father, "No man, I take my Big Mama with me. Because Big Mama's heart beats Andries."

It was then we heard more Spaniards enter our home. Sounds of destruction and demolition were going on. I heard a certain man was saying, "The girl is in here somewhere. She is hiding the knight and the dead writer and his half-dead wife somewhere in here. We can just demolish the whole Kasteel Vrederic and bury all the living and dead spirits once and for all. I don't believe this castle is haunted but it's that girl who is a real witch. Her grandmother too is a witch. The writer was a nobleman and a preacher who died just to protect those two witches. I don't understand what the knight saw in her. He fell in love with her. I guess his great-granduncle who had sent him was also bewitched like him by the witches. Burn the house down and all shall be good eradication."

Then we heard another man come and stand next to us as for the very first time I saw the honorable knight, Sir Alexander van der Bijl, stand in front of us. I touched his hands as without thinking I tried to protect him from being seen. Yet he stared at me in astonishment and said, "Dear Sir, is it really you? Are you here in spirit form? Or is my fever getting to my head? For if it is you, then know I will keep, protect, and save the honor of your granddaughter to my last breath. I will fight and free this blessed home of all thugs."

I held on to him without any challenges and was able to take him inside to the hidden chamber. With the help of all the other spirit family members, we were able to take a very tall six-foot-four-inch, black-haired, green-eyed man watching me like we had always met like this. I realized he was a soldier and real knight and was used to facing all different circumstances.

We placed the knight on the ground on top of fresh towels and I knew I must undress him and see to his wounds. I called Rietje without remembering about our time differences and told her, "Rietje come here and help Opa please. Open my little bookcase we had made. Remember? It has a bag hidden in there. Bring it to me sweetheart."

She came as she followed my words. She opened my secret bookcase and brought my medical bag I had stored just before my travels through the mystical door of dreams. She stood next to me and tried to hug me yet her hands went right through my body. It felt funny but I realized she could see me. For the first time I realized with my call, she was given the permission to see me.

I told Sir Alexander, "I am a doctor who will only try to help you, not hurt you. I will do with things available to me within my hands."

I watched Rietje bring the things as she did get my message. She was a very smart woman even in the seventeenth century. I watched Mama and Papa as they were both looking in the opposite direction, so Mama who had a weak heart toward the sight of blood would not faint.

I told my mother, "It's all right. He is all good to go. I am glad we have antibiotics as he has an infection. It will be all right in a few days. Rietje, you can take care of him. I will write everything down. Don't skip any medications."

I watched Rietje as she said, "Opa is it really you? Can you please fix up Oma? I am worried as she sleeps a lot with a high fever. She did this to herself as she tried to kill the person who shot Opa. It was like a thunderbolt had happened, and someone shot Opa in the heart. Opa fell and never got up yet Oma went out with her stones and threw as much as she could while she got shot multiple times as she stood in between. I ran after them but Oma tied me up in the secret library and said not to come out until Sir Alexander returns."

I watched Sir Alexander awaken and say, "I returned to only be thrown a sword in the back. Oma had brought us in here. I saw Rietje was kept in here safely as she had gotten herself free when she went out to fight by herself. I did as Oma said and have kept her hidden in here, waiting for a miracle as I asked the Lover's Lighthouse to save the love of my life and her grandparents."

I watched Rietje as I did walk over to check Margriete and she saw me and said, "Please don't separate from me. I want to be with you only."

I did check both my own self and Margriete and knew I was too late and could not do anything. I remained quiet as I could not take Margriete's pain.

My mother came in front of everyone and said, "How did you two get to know one another? I never got to read your full story. By the way, I am your Great-Oma, reincarnated wife of your Great-Opa Johannes van Vrederic. My name in that time period was Mahalt. I know my name was unknown to all of you as my beloved husband had lost his memories due to my early death."

I realized Mama was trying to divert Rietje's attention away from here. Rietje watched and Mama said, "Your Great-Opa Johannes is here too. I had sent you our diaries from the future. I hope one day when you are lonely and need something to hold on to, then my sweetheart, do open the pages and read them. We will always be with you through these pages."

Papa came forward and introduced himself and said, "My dear I am your Great-Opa here with your Opa and your Papa. We are all here in the same house. Our home, your home. For it is our responsibility to make sure no one takes away your home from you. For throughout time, you shall have this home as your home. For when the time comes when someone takes our house away from us, it is then I shall be reborn to buy our home back all over again. These are my vows from the beyond."

Rietje started to cry and said, "I wish Oma could have seen all of this. I am afraid she has slipped away from us."

It was then I walked toward my Margriete again to see if she really had slipped away and realized she too was falling asleep. She looked like she was all drained out yet she still had her amazing, beautiful gaze in her eyes that had captured the heart of the then sixteenth-century Jacobus. She still had the gaze and would entrap the twenty-first-century Jacobus. I watched her sleeping peacefully on top of my other physical body. I laughed and thought to myself, woman you were heavy and had always slept on top of me while I was alive and today as my body lies asleep you still lie on top of me. You really won't let me go alone I understand.

I watched Margriete say, "Jacobus don't move me okay. I will never let you go. In life or in death. For how could I be alive if you are no more? Also Jacobus I am a jealous wife, so I am worried what if you fall for another woman where you have traveled to? Now my husband, why do you look like a ghost if I am still here left behind?"

Her words were whispers and I realized they were her last words. As she held on to him, she looked up at me and said, "Don't you become a spirit if I still am not. You dare try to be young and handsome when I am still old and fragile. Remember if you are a bird flying around in the skies, then I will be the cage you must come and settle within. If you become the everlasting lights in the skies, I will be your glory. My love, take me away with you. For how could I still be here if you have moved on? My evermore beloved, I shall never let you go."

I started to break down as I watched Margriete was slowly slipping away. She watched me and said, "Don't you dare cry for me and be weak. For I am sleeping on top of you. Never shall I let you go. Tie a ribbon on my hands and yours so we don't ever separate. Also when we get onto the Ferris wheel together, don't you let me fall off anywhere other than where you are. As in my dreams we were separated. I fell off and I asked you, 'Would you recognize me if I come in a different form with a new face in a different time?' I will hold on to this line throughout time as a testament of our love, when I see you again. I see all of the family members have arrived riding the wagon of karma, then please set free our home, the besieged Kasteel Vrederic."

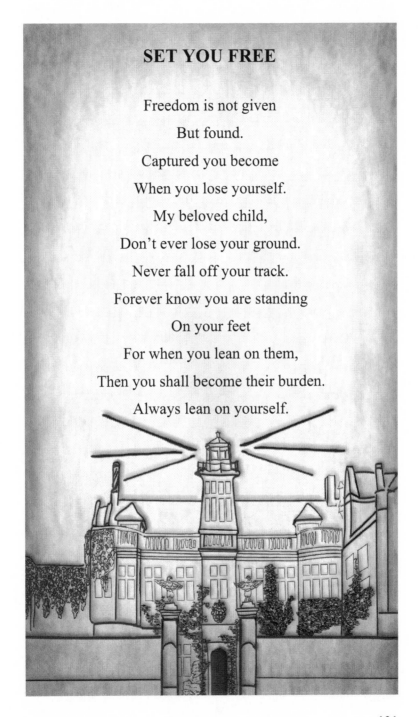

SET YOU FREE

Freedom is not given

But found.

Captured you become

When you lose yourself.

My beloved child,

Don't ever lose your ground.

Never fall off your track.

Forever know you are standing

On your feet

For when you lean on them,

Then you shall become their burden.

Always lean on yourself.

Be the one who finds your ground.

Never let another person take your ground.

Forever know

Behind you follow the spirits of the truth.

Hold on to the truth and

Watch how the truth holds on to you.

Don't let them capture you

Within the wagon of lies

For you shall always

Hold on to the scales of the truth

Which shall guarantee you

Your freedom and always

SET YOU FREE.

My Treasured Child,

Forever walk upon the path of the truth and honesty as they shall always be your victory speech. Truth shall always set you free from the wrong. Never fall prey to the powerful wrong. Never fear the powerful voice of the wrong for they have lost their path and will not even know they are the lost travelers. For always ask yourself how could a lost traveler guide the other travelers back onto the right path, if they themselves have never walked upon it?

I have seen the powerful wrong are always loud and noisy. It's because they actually lack the knowledge yet they like all the people around them to think they are filled with knowledge. These unjust people besiege things and even humans that don't belong to them.

It is strange as they should be taught they cannot imprison a bird that belongs in the free and not in a cage. For it is only time they can take away from the bird. For at the first chance of an exit, the bird will fly out of the cage.

She will fly to be with her own family and friends. You cannot force someone or something to be yours, if it does not belong to you. For how could a person imprison a person's soul, or his or her inner love if it is not even there?

A person who can think for herself will free herself from all the forceful imprisonments at the first available moment. My child never let anyone keep you or your intelligent mind in a prison. Be free from all bondages of the wrongful might or minds. Remember always do as your heart guides you, for your heart shall never lie. For within your inner heart you shall find the complete truth of your mind.

Ask yourself the questions you seek answers to. I believe the answers will be found within your own self, your own heart. Your heart shall always guide you to the right and prevent you from taking the wrong step. Your knowledge toward what your heart desires in life shall set you free.

Love always,

Opa

CHAPTER SEVEN:

The Invisible War

"Sometimes you can see your opponents, yet if you cannot see them, does it mean they don't exist?"

*The Invisible War begins with the women from the
sacred Kasteel Vrederic teaching the assailants a lesson
they will never forget.*

R ainy day brought upon Kasteel Vrederic even more tears that were pouring yet needed to be clogged. For I wondered if I could not clog my tears then how would I teach my granddaughter to stop crying when I am again gone? She would lose me twice as now she had all of us in front of her even in spirit form. I only wondered could the castle become alive and be with my precious granddaughter when we would all be gone? The thought of separation from her was killing me inside.

Papa came and sat next to me as we both were trying to think how we could get our home back. Papa said, "It's killing me inside too, as I know we must leave and separate from our beloved Rietje. The worst part is how do we leave her here and move on? She is devastated by the death of her Opa and her Oma who is following him. Yet how do we physically and spiritually separate from her?"

I watched Mama, Katelijne, and Griet come and sit in the crowd. I knew Rietje was still in the secret room locked in hiding with Sir Alexander and the two bodies waiting to leave this Earth. I knew something was still keeping my physical body dead yet somewhat alive. There still was a pulse so I could not declare myself dead. Yet I wondered what was it that kept both of them lagging behind?

I wished I could do something and awaken them like magic. I felt like why did I become a doctor if I can't save all lives?

Antonius said, "What cannot be changed should be left alone. Yet the destiny we can change should be paid attention to. We are all lagging behind because we are all emotionally drained. Yet if we awaken from our dreams before we can be of help to my grandniece, then our journey would have been in vain."

I watched the great soldier Theunis had arrived and said, "My daughter is a soldier like her father. She can take care of herself. I know the journey of life is hard yet if we can give her home back to her, she will always have the diaries to travel through at the time of her need or will. Kasteel Vrederic is alive and all of us will be here throughout time. She will have all of her ancestors and future lineage living here together through the walls of the castle. Yet now we must help her fight this war to get back the castle and make it her home."

I watched my brother Antonius watch over his shoulders as even in spirit form, he knew something was amiss. We all knew his sixth sense was sensing some kind of trouble. We all tried to listen and heard men talking in groups. There were horses and carriages that had arrived with new people in the Kasteel Vrederic courtyard.

We all went quiet as Mama ran inside with Andries and Katelijne. They told me they would try to be on guard if anyone tries to get into the secret library. I watched my granddaughter Rietje and Sir Alexander silently walk inside the secret room as they saw Mama had signaled them to hide. There were so many armed soldiers coming inside the castle, it felt like the castle was already their residence.

An army general walked in from one of the carriages as he told his subordinate officers, "Are the women ready? How many women did you get as prisoners? We can't let anyone know about our illegal business of selling young women. They must all be brought here and then transported around the country to soldiers. We will just say they were all caught stealing and robbing innocent people. We will also say they were cursing farmers' crops and vegetation. The new arrivals can all be charged with killing farm animals through strange curses and poisonings. The witch burnings have been stopped yet we will say they were caught red-handed so they must be tried and imprisoned as either sex slaves or as we see the punishments to be fitting for their crimes."

We all stood up as did Papa and we knew the witch burnings and heretical crimes had not stopped even though publicly they were said to have been stopped. The women were unjustly being treated and anyone speaking against the captors would too be punished. We saw there were a lot of men who too were brought in as they tried to save their wives and daughters. A neighbor's jealousy or envy of another neighbor was enough to bring forth false accusations against one another.

I knew we must again do something to save the honor of all the women who were brought as prisoners to our home. No one will be harmed in our home. I watched Katelijne watch all of this and knew this was a very touchy subject on her part.

Yet she stood there like a warrior and said, "I will finish this war on my terms and set all the innocent women and men free. For this is an invisible war. I can see you the culprit, yet you can't see me. So let this war begin."

Mama watched us and said, "My great-granddaughter's honor will be be kept intact, as we the members of the Kasteel Vrederic family will never allow any unjust to take place in this home. Like I told all of you, I will be the mother of my children, yet I will be like a snake goddess and keep all the enemies away from my family and lineage. I was taught by my Indian grandmother, my Nani, not to fear danger but to be the danger."

I quickly walked back to see if my little Rietje was okay. I entered the room where I saw Sir Alexander calming her down. He was patting her back and told her, "My beauty you are my field of wildflowers. I know you planted forget-me-nots all around your home with your Opa yet touch my chest and you will see the wildflower field is growing in here only for you. I have not crossed all the oceans and lands searching for the most beautiful woman to be separated from you, but to find you. In my eyes, you will find all the love you need. Within my inner soul, you will find your everlasting beloved. My entranced beloved, I shall never let you go as I have been enchanted by your love. Forever I shall keep you safe."

My little granddaughter was crying and she said, "I can fight all my battles. I am not afraid of the men or goons yet if only Opa was with me. I don't know if I can even survive a day without him, yet how will I live without him? Sir Alexander, I am worried not about the goons but how will I allow my Opa to be left alone outside in the garden all by himself in the cold? Also Oma is scared of the rain and the thundering storms. They are fragile and need me now. My Opa raised me all by himself and never let me feel like I was an orphan. After Oma came, I always slept on her chest, even now as an old maiden I still sleep with my head buried in Oma's chest, as Oma rubs my temples until I fall asleep. Now who will rub my temples?"

Sir Alexander watched Rietje and said, "When you take the oath and be my bride, I promise from then onward, I shall rub your temples just like your Oma. For her and in her memory, I shall keep my promise to never be upset at you before bed and take care of you until my last breath."

I felt my mother's hands on my shoulders as I ran outside worrying about my brave little granddaughter who was not worried about the goons outside but about the separation all humans must go through. Also I was overjoyed with happiness to see with my own eyes what a blessed life partner she had found.

Papa came around and said, "Let's worry about how we are going to get all the goons out of our home. Let's not invite them in but kick the uninvited goons out. Yet my son remember time heals everything and I promise you as soon as we go back to our time period, I will find Margriete and my Griet and you can work on your Rietje."

Theunis and Griet came and Theunis told us, "The goons are taking all the captive women to the carriage house. They have decided these women are not good enough to be kept inside Kasteel Vrederic. Yet we have found amongst the women a very old woman who too was brought in with these women. Jacobus, I have brought her inside through the secret door. She could see me as clear as I could see her. She is waiting outside with Antonius and Katelijne to meet you. It seems somehow Antonius had met her before."

I was shocked as was Papa as we both said at the same time, "That's not possible as we are from different time periods."

Mama watched me for a while as she smiled and so did I while Papa only watched in surprise as he asked, "Why are you all smiling and how come I don't get the joke or mystery?"

Mama and I said in union, "Aunt Marinda is here."

That's when we saw in front of us was standing in the courtyard Aunt Marinda. Her white hair was shining in the light and her eyes were bright as ever. She saw me and hugged me for a long time.

She then said, "My child, my Jacobus, how could you think our Rietje would be in trouble and I would not arrive? Like I told you, I would watch over Kasteel Vrederic eternally. If any member of this family ever needs me or is in pain, I will arrive before you can even call my name, that too in whatever century you all might be in."

Antonius was standing there as he said, "We met as I was guided by this blessed woman to my Katelijne. I will not even ask how you can travel from time to time. Yet I know Big Mama said you are the time traveler who had taken a vow to be with or around Jacobus eternally."

She watched me for a while as she knew my rock-solid eyes too would pour out with her in sight. She told me, "Jacobus, let's get this home goon-free and get you back to your time period, for there I promise someone is waiting for you. I actually just left her over there. A very sweet woman. Yet I will stay back in this time period until my Rietje has her children. Her triplets are going to need someone to take care of them. Someone young and strong like myself."

I heard her message, my Rietje will have triplets. I guess it ran in the family because my paternal grandmother was a triplet. I watched this blessed woman's face as she was watching me carefully contemplating my every thought. I reassured her with a wink I am okay now for she just gave me the only leash that will keep me going.

It was then we heard screams outside. Fearful women's painful screams ripped the air as my family members all watched Theunis for guidance. We saw Sir Alexander, the brave knight, had walked near us and told us, "I want to help too, for I would not be able to live with myself if any one of the women is hurt in this home, a home

Opa, Jacobus van Vrederic, has left in my care, alongside his only granddaughter."

I watched Theunis say, "You keep my daughter safe for now as I will make sure these goons run out of this home before tomorrow comes. I know I would be blessed to have a son-in-law like you Sir Alexander. I would want this home to always be protected for my future generations and your future generations. So if these goons don't leave, I promise for all of them, tomorrow shall never be. They attacked my father-in-law and my mother-in-law whom I had promised to protect throughout time. Yet for some reason we were stuck traveling between time while they attacked."

Theunis watched all of us and said, "Family members who can't be seen, let's begin our attack. First let's take away all of their weapons and then let's move on to them and maybe we can start tying them up. I want all of you to know you can do all of this at your will as you don't want to harm anyone but only protect our own family."

Mama watched him and said, "I won't harm anyone but I will bite all who come and try to bite my great-granddaughter or any other woman."

I watched Griet and Katelijne both look into the thin air as both were scared of the goons. I knew Katelijne had her own fears as she was a rape victim herself.

Papa followed my eyes as he said, "Griet you are my brave granddaughter and I know you too can fight these useless goons who prey on innocent victims even during a war they are trying to win. Katelijne, my daughter, you are brave and strong. You fought death all by yourself and now you have your whole family fighting with you. I know you can do it."

Katelijne said, "I was a victim yet I survived only because a brave doctor and his brothers had intervened. Today I have one of the brothers as my husband, my twin flame, the other in his reincarnated form as my son, and one of the brothers as my big brother. I will fight for all other women who too are fighting for their honor. No I am not afraid and I will not allow any trigger effects to take away time I could fight for any and all other victims. I am blessed as today I stand with a blessed family and I promise, I shall never let you go."

Rietje walked near us and said, "It's not going to be hard as you all are invisible and they are all visible. It's true you should never attack someone from the back, yet they attacked my Opa, my Oma, and Sir Alexander from the back. If we don't stop them, they will kill me and take over my family home and take away the honor of so many young women all within our home. My Opa said not to go and ever attack verbally or physically someone else in their own homes. Yet today they have come and for no reason attacked my family from the back."

I told them all, "We shall not attack or harm anyone but only remove our enemies from our property. This house is rumored to be haunted. I understand that is one of the reasons they have invaded our property. I do wonder what would happen if they had to come face-to-face with the ghosts of Kasteel Vrederic. As I understand, the spirits belong in this house as this castle is their home, yet these goons do not belong in our property. They are the invaders, so we will declare a war where we can see the enemy as we are the spirits who own the home. Yet they won't be able to see us as they are the invaders trying to forcefully enter. As the son of the property owner of the sixteenth-century Kasteel Vrederic and again the son of the twenty-first-century Kasteel Vrederic owner, this is our war. I declare this war on behalf of my family. I call it the Invisible War."

VISIBLE TO THE HEART

My love remains with you forever.

You can't see it,

Nor can you touch it,

Yet it has been sent

From my heartbeats

To your heartbeats

As a granddaughter

And her grandfather

Are forever invisibly

Connected through only

Our heartbeats for one another.

When you miss me my child

Because you can't see me

Or maybe I am too far away,

Remember even then

I am and shall always be

Felt within your heartbeats.

For my love for you

And your love for me

Is eternal even though it is

Invisible to the human eyes

Yet infinitely visible to the receiver's heart

Which beats my name,

For my heartbeat

Forever recites your name.

As everyone says love is invisible

Yet remember my dear,

It is,

VISIBLE TO THE HEART.

My Beloved Rietje,

Forever my love will be with you. Like the spirits of Kasteel Vrederic, it can't be seen but only felt by you. Sweet granddaughter always know when I find it impossible to breathe without you around me, I keep on reminding myself but you are always here with me, through my tears and within all the joys of life I know your memories are reflected.

Today I would ask you to not ever fall prey to anyone by showing your weakness by letting the tears fall and closing your sight even for a minute. If tears fall out of control in front of the unjust, then do remember the joys and good time we had together as a family. If ever you find yourself in a war zone, keep your eyes open even for the invisible enemies you can feel yet can't see. For remember it's always not those whom you can see but those whom you cannot see that might become a threat.

People who become ignorant and refuse to see the truth in front of them only shall fall off the path. For in life, we must also use our sixth sense as I was taught by your granduncle who was born blind. He had to sense everything around himself to protect himself from the unseen enemies he had to live with. He taught us about the human competence of having the sixth sense, just like we automatically shut our eyes if we see an insect coming toward us.

Your granduncle was born with his sixth sense as a gift from the beyond. So even today as he does have his sight, he still uses his sixth sense as we all do. For when a person's sight, hearing, taste, smell, or touch fail, it is then a person must rely on his or her sixth sense as a person's sixth sense never lies.

It is your sixth sense that takes you toward the knowledge that would have been invisible otherwise. Forever my child, keep an eye out for your visible and invisible enemies, with your sixth sense.

Love you always,

Opa

CHAPTER EIGHT:

Kasteel Vrederic Is Haunted

"If a home could only talk, she would let you know who she belongs to, or who she wants as her family members. That's where the saying, 'a house calls you' comes from."

*Erasmus van Phillip and Antonius van Phillip from the
twenty-first century, join their seventeenth-century
family members to liberate their home from tyrants,
even crossing time.*

I was drowning in grief as all I wanted to do was awaken Margriete and let everything freeze back in time. I watched my Rietje and her beloved knight, Sir Alexander, watch one another with so much love, it made all my inner sorrows disappear. If only I could have bottled up all the love stories and spread them like a perfume in the air, maybe this world would have had less problems and sorrows. Yet I knew tonight I only wanted this world to stay quiet as my beloved Margriete was sleeping ever so peacefully on top of my lifeless body.

I watched her from the fog I was in and asked her, "My sweetheart why do you love me so much that it hurts to even let you go for a minute? How do I leave you alone in the open air where I know you will be scared? How do I leave Rietje alone in the hands of a man I barely know? What if she needs me? What do I do? Someone please make some sense in all of this. Margriete answer my questions please."

I saw my daughter Griet was standing at the corner of the room. She came near me and said, "Papa I know we have not seen one another other than I being a spirit and you in physical form. Yet did that stop you from loving me? Did you not love me Papa, even though we were separated by time and fog?"

I watched my brave child and hugged her for I was able to hug her as we were both in spirit form. I felt blessed to be able to do this. I knew we must move on and begin our invisible war against the enemies who had made our home into their camp. Then I saw my whole family was standing and watching over me. I saw my brave Rietje watching over me as she just wiped her tears.

She watched me for a while and said, "Opa I know you probably do remember or maybe not, yet you were the one who introduced me to Sir Alexander the Knight. You told me my knight in shining armor would come to take me away, far away from you. I told you if he does want me to go far away, then I will declare war with him as this is my home. Nothing or no one will take me away from my home."

She watched her knight and continued, "Yet he never came to take me away but only protect our family from harm's way. As a knight in all of the King's lands, he knew our home was under siege and he had promised Sir Krijn, his great-granduncle, he would protect our home from the Spaniards or the Dutch Resistance Army. Whoever attacks our home would be his enemy."

I knew the story as I do remember how my little girl had grown up in front of my eyes and become a woman as she found her knight in shining armor. She fell head over heels in love with him as he did with her. I blessed them and told them if he could prove to me he loves her more than anything else in this world, then I would happily agree to give her hands in marriage to him.

I told everyone, "I do remember I am blessed to have him as a member of the family. I know after we all leave, you still will have a happy home with him. Now you also have Aunt Marinda who will be staying over here with you."

Everyone was quiet as we heard more gunshots and screams of women who were being tortured by unjust men. We got up and knew it was time for the world to know, we would not accept any unjust in our home.

I told everyone, "Come on everyone, let's prove to this world a house has her mind and knows who she wants as her family. She knows who she wants residing within her walls. If only the walls could talk, they would let you know if the house wants you or not. Let's go and let the enemy camp know our home is not their camp but our haven where they are not welcome. Let our house talk to them and let them know some houses can talk and this is one such home, where she will choose her owners not the other way around."

I watched everyone as Theunis said, "Jacobus means we are all going to haunt the enemy soldiers and show them some real-life ghost stories, even their children will recite to their grandchildren. As Jacobus never hurts anyone nor would he take a life as a doctor from the twenty-first century, his oath is to save lives. Similar to his sixteenth-century self as a preacher, he had said he would not take any life but only teach all to protect one another. So we scare them off of their own pants, literally."

I watched Rietje walk toward her father and say, "I want to be included in this group, even though I am not fortunate enough to be a ghost."

Katelijne walked toward her and said, "I am your grandaunt and I command you to take back what you just said. Young woman you must stay alive so I can become your grandaunt. For remember without you, none of us exist. Also in due time, I too will be there when you young woman will take care of this old grandaunt. Until then, do believe in miracles and the door of reincarnation which comes after death. So nothing to be afraid of. Also in this life you are blessed to have such a wonderful twin flame who will be there for you throughout eternity. Hey Rietje, we need more details about your romantic journey with Sir Alexander. I want to retell my future generations. Big Mama wanted me to ask so I ask."

My mother watched everyone and said, "Okay it's true, I wanted more juicy details from Rietje and Sir

Alexander's love story. We will always be here with you through the home we all share even in different time periods. For remember we all have this home as a bridge in between. So let's all go and bite some enemies as I am ready to bite my enemies and then we can all enjoy our Rietje and Sir Alexander's love story."

Papa walked up to Mama and said, "My beloved wife, please no biting as I would like my wife to be with me eternally as a human or a spirit not a vampire. Without you, I too was known as a man without any heart in my previous life. Yet for you I became a lover and for you I became a father as without you I had your son but was lost in a world of nothingness. So let's all be safe and know with time you shall all find your twin flames. My son's twin flame awaits him so we must all not get lost. Also I too want more details about my great-granddaughter and Sir Alexander's love story."

My precious granddaughter was glowing from either being shy or in love. I watched her and knew it was both. The night was still young as lanterns were all glowing in the dark and the seventeenth-century castle was glowing in the bright moonlit night. We all knew we would go as a group and start our job in the night yet continue in the daylight hours. We would prove to them these ghosts don't quit even in the daylight.

As we crossed the huge gardens and walked into the carriage house, we saw women were all tied up in groups. I stepped into the carriage house where I had first made love to Margriete, where my journey into becoming a father had begun. The most beautiful night in my life remained just a memory. Yet I will keep the memories alive and I took a vow, never will I allow any sin to take place in this sacred house.

We did allow Rietje to accompany us as did Sir Alexander the Knight. Everyone only saw Rietje and her beloved knight approaching them. They were all laughing as they thought my granddaughter and her knight were surrendering to them in fear. The whole castle grounds felt like a prison sentence for women and some very fragile and elderly men. They had campfires lit all around and small groups of men were eating at the campsite. One would actually think there was some kind of a retreat going on. Yet only the men sitting at the campsite were laughing and seemed to be having fun.

I watched the cruel army tease my granddaughter. As they saw her, they all started to laugh and say, "Do you want to join the women and become one of them now? We see you have come to your senses. Oh and your wounded knight is with you to get wounded again. So why not just be a part of our group? We need a knight like you, and always would love to have a woman of your beauty and grace with us."

Aunt Marinda who followed us replied, "No, we don't want to be a part of your group but actually we are witches who have come to find food for our wild dogs. We would love to have some hunting games as we love to hunt at night. Yet we can continue even through the daylight hours as we don't need to sleep like you all. Tonight dear devil warriors, we would love to take your pants off and feed your private parts to our hungry dogs. They have had no food for so long. They are even more hungry than your wildest warrior."

I watched the men break out in a laughter as then they said, "We know there are no such things as witches. We have imprisoned all of these women with lies. So don't try to fool us as you are the fool who now will be our prisoner too."

I watched the big general with a huge stomach and a very shiny bald head which reflected the light, walk out of the tent as he was laughing with joy now the castle was theirs to keep. Then Mama got up and I knew she was up to something as I watched her go and take off the general's pants and leave him with only his undergarments in front of all to see. He started to get his guns ready to shoot at Rietje and Sir Alexander when I watched my brother and Papa go around like a fog and remove all of their guns and throw them into the fire. It caused a huge bonfire which had lit the night skies even higher.

The warriors of the enemy camp were all trying to handle a disaster zone as they could not see their enemies, yet we saw them clear as day. It was then I watched Katelijne run into the carriage house as she released one woman after another and whispered into their ears, a funny phrase.

She said, "We are the spirits of Kasteel Vrederic and we have been living here for centuries. We can bite and eat all of you up if you only misbehave. We shall set all innocent free yet will bite all evil forever during your lifetime. However, you must never do wrong that was done unto you. Forever only do right by all, or else you shall find yourself as a prisoner again. You will see us if you are evil as our bite is more dangerous than a poisonous snake."

I observed Mama start to hiss as she said, "I will bite all the men as they want to bite all the women, so let's bite off their manly parts first."

We just sat and watched our women go wild and pull the pants off of all men and left them in their undergarments. The women also placed scorching charcoals in the men's clothing to burn them from inside their private places. The soldiers started to run in all different directions as they watched their pants come off. They were worried how this was happening as they could not see their enemies.

Sir Alexander and Rietje stood there with their swords and started to battle all men who dared to come near them. I watched a proud father, Theunis, walk by his daughter at all times as did Griet who said out loud, "This is my daughter. Come and fight with her sword. You will be cut into pieces and fed to our castle hounds as they want revenge for your cowardly actions against the most honorable nobleman in the region. You attacked a nobleman and his blessed wife so you could imprison women and have sex with them in our home. Not in this life or any other as the nobleman you attacked is standing right here watching all of you as a spirit. Much stronger than the weak and old man you cowards had attacked."

The night had gone by fast as all around, the news had spread about how the spirits of Kasteel Vrederic were angry as the noble diarist and his wife were murdered mercilessly. Yet he now stood in his castle as a spirit and would protect his home throughout time. Now any enemy who tried to get in here would be defeated by the spirits as revenge.

My baby nephew Andries too was being carried around by his grandfather, my Papa, as Papa told him, "No one in this family will sit back if our family and home is ever attacked again. It took a great noble diarist like Jacobus van Vrederic and his beloved wife Margriete to die to get this freedom. No one will ever dare to come and attack our family in our own home. A home is a person's safe haven."

It took us all night to get rid of most of the enemies and then we set all the captured victims free. The risk was high as they tried to shoot at Rietje and her beloved knight but both were well-trained fighters who if not outnumbered could have kept the castle safe on their own. The army was numbered in hundreds of unjust men who called themselves soldiers yet we called them nothing more than wild animals who were looking for innocent victims as their prey.

All the fighters in the enemy camp were fighting to keep Kasteel Vrederic as their prisoner camp. It was then Theunis had asked me to show myself to all of the enemies for just a few seconds and disappear like a fog. He had asked me to let all of the enemies know they had killed Jacobus van Vrederic yet they shall never get rid of him from his own home.

So I appeared like a spirit ever so clearly in front of all of them. I told them, "You are the mighty powerful wrong. I shall avenge your wrong as long as you live for I know you are all just cowardly bullies. In a war, there should always be fair and square treatments. Yet I see here you have created a torture camp for the innocent victims. I will not allow my home to become your victim and be known as a torture camp. So I warn you to leave or as I could not physically save myself, I vow from the beyond I shall spiritually save my home and see to it that every single one of you is brutally punished."

Morning came very quickly when we saw our home Kasteel Vrederic was free. Every single one of the remaining enemy soldiers left like thunderbolts. Rumors too spread like wildfires as the sixteenth-century Jacobus van Vrederic was killed alongside his beloved wife by the unjust brutal enemies of the Dutch Eighty Years' War and the unjust witch burnings he objected to.

Dawn was shining upon the home where I knew my sixteenth and seventeenth-century body had passed away peacefully. I watched on top of my earthly body laid Margriete's sixteenth and seventeenth-century lifeless body. Our seventeenth-century family members and our twenty-first-century family members were all holding on to one another, as we knew this was the end of a diary yet the beginning of another one. My family members started to retell all about our love stories from eternally beloved, evermore beloved, be my destiny, heart beats your name, and entranced beloved to one another. This family promised to never let go of one another as we promised in life or in death, we shall always be together through our home Kasteel Vrederic.

I knew our home would be safe forever as our home now shall be known as the most haunted home in the area. The morning dawn also left sad feelings within the walls of our home as now our home would forever be known as a haunted house. I felt empty and hollow somehow inside. My home, the house my father had remodeled and bought back over and over again to keep within our family, would be known as the most haunted home. I had a hard time digesting this information.

My mother watched all of us and said, "Jacobus, go find the bathroom please. I understand we are in our dream tunnel, yet you guys do understand it would be nice to know we have a bathroom as I searched all over the castle for one and I still can't seem to find one. Usually I keep on searching for one and wake up from my dreams. I know this is different. Still, I hope there is one. In my dreams, I use the bathroom. In some dreams, I do cook and eat. Also sometimes your Papa gets me drunk too."

I wondered if Mama understood we were in the seventeenth century. I told her, "Our home during the seventeenth century had outhouses for toilets and wooden tubs where water would be brought in for bathing. In the safe house, I do remember I had brought in a chamber pot and a small wooden tub installed for emergency situations."

Mama watched everyone and said, "Erasmus come with me. Let's go outside."

Papa only said, "Yes dear."

Papa then came and held me from the back as he said, "My son remember within all negativity and bad giving, something good always comes out of it. The house I had built was lost during the time it passed on from one family member to the other. Yet even when I had repurchased our home, it was vacant for a long time. The only reason I was able to repurchase it back from the bank for our family was, because it was rumored to have been haunted. It's all good because we will make sure people know this is our home. With all the sorrows of death and the joys of rebirth, our home is just that, our home."

A person can't forcibly get into a home without being called an intruder or even buy a home if the home does not open her doors to you. Forever people call their houses their properties, yet forget we are the inhabitants of the house.

Even though time passes by us, the inhabitants of all homes actually share the walls of a home who keeps all the stories of her home a secret, buried within her walls which live there eternally.

So I always remembered my house had shared her walls with me then in the past with my granddaughter, in the present, and again myself in the future. I realized all houses have their own mind and so it's true the house picks her owners and our home had picked our family as her inhabitants. I heard all around the Spanish army and the Dutch Resistance Army were saying, "Don't go near that house! The house is bloody haunted!"

So the rumors started to spread faster than even wildfires could spread that Kasteel Vrederic is haunted.

OUR HOME

Cherished granddaughter

Who is my heartbeat,

Remember your home

Is your haven.

The walls

Are your secret diaries.

The floor

Is your evergreen field.

The memories left behind are reminiscences

That shall be alive

If only you believe.

Close your eyes

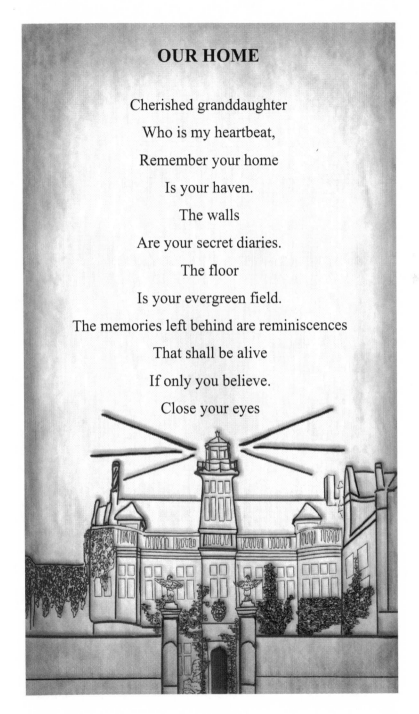

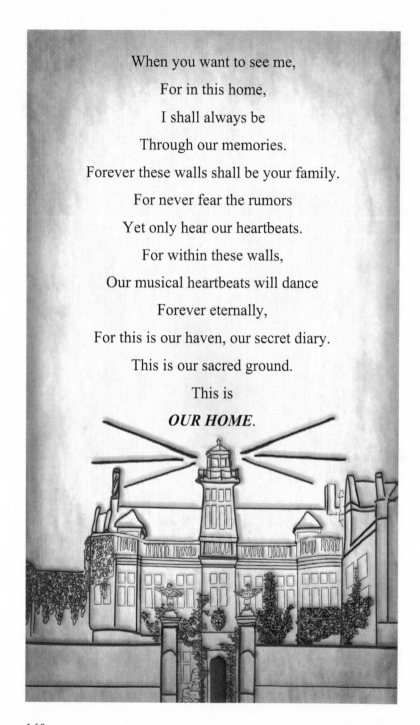

When you want to see me,

For in this home,

I shall always be

Through our memories.

Forever these walls shall be your family.

For never fear the rumors

Yet only hear our heartbeats.

For within these walls,

Our musical heartbeats will dance

Forever eternally,

For this is our haven, our secret diary.

This is our sacred ground.

This is

OUR HOME.

My Beloved Granddaughter of the Seventeenth Century,

Remember our home is not haunted by ghosts but rather blessed through the memories our house is blessed to have within her walls. This house was built by your ancestors and even in the twenty-first century, she still belongs in our family. The blessed home is a sacred ground where remember during the yesteryears your Oma and I had raised you. Within the walls of this home are hidden your ancestral chronicles.

Today again through the door of reincarnation, my Mama, your Great-Oma, and my Papa, your Great-Opa, have raised my brothers and me. I had watched my nephew too walk on this sacred ground you had learned to walk on during the sixteenth century. So remember always this is a blessed home and is no way haunted.

For I would ask all the rumor spreaders, why is it they fear a body sleeping in the cold open grass so much, when they did not fear the same person while he or she had so lovingly laid in the same bed with them and had shared the same dinner table with them just maybe yesterday?

My child don't fear the dead as they only sleep outside but fear the wrongful mouth of the wrong who spread rumors yet forget. As they haunted this world with rumors today, tomorrow they shall be feared by their own family members as they too join the dead. Let this world know today they are alive as this is their present. Yet if tomorrow they are no more, then would not their hearts desire their memories to be kept alive? That's called a blessing not haunting. My child always know all the homes across this globe had someone living in them once upon a time. Yet they have passed after their time on Earth was over, leaving behind histories not hauntings. Our home is blessed with historical memories and love.

Signed your beloved,

Opa

CHAPTER NINE:

Defeated By The Spirits Of Kasteel Vrederic

"Rumors spread faster than fires can burn, so even though time passes by, the rumors of a house being haunted remain through the fearful minds of the humans, or the saying just might be true, 'Where there is some rumor, there is some truth.'"

*The family members of Kasteel Vrederic defend their
home from the unjust invaders, even across time.*

awn reached the seventeenth-century Kasteel Vrederic with a sudden realization of sorrow and grief. A clear winter morning with just the perfect amount of warm sunlight streamed through the windows. The sparkling rays of the morning sun were beautiful as Mama had made fresh breakfast in the seventeenth-century Kasteel Vrederic. She made it seem so very easy. Everyone thought she was part of the seventeenth-century inhabitants, by the graceful way she handled everything.

I watched Aunt Marinda had kept herself busy speaking with Mama. Griet and Katelijne were busy with Andries as he was busy exploring all the missing rooms of the castle. The little boy would walk into a wall crying for his playroom to appear. Papa was having so much fun with the boy as he was teasing Andries to find the missing rooms. Andries cried and told Mama, "Big Mama, Big Papa said he ate my room. I can't find my toys and my big bear."

Mama came in and scooped up the child as she kissed his head and calmed him down. Papa said, "That's not fair, I was having so much fun with him. He can't understand why his home is the same yet different. He keeps on repeating 'find room' and runs off to find his room. Then he asked, 'Big Papa did you eat Andries's room? Now find it.'"

I saw Aunt Marinda say, "Grow up Johannes. You are an adult now. At least it's good you have changed and it seems you love children."

Papa watched her and said, "Yes Aunt Marinda, I have grown up and am Erasmus now. Because I have my wife, I do understand I was a bitter man who only missed her and could not think of anything else. The world is full of love when I have her. Yet I do realize my son Jacobus made the world a loving place for all around him, even by being miserable inside. He never let this come in between his family and him. I only wish I could have been there for him in the sixteenth century with all my memories intact."

I held on to Papa and told him, "Papa I visited your room and saw how much you had missed Mama. I only wish I could have known the full story, then I too could have helped. It was amazing how you never let your miseries touch me, yet they still did, so it is better to share and not keep them inside. I guess we are all learning."

I heard Antonius and Theunis and Sir Alexander break out into a laughing fit as Andries was haunting the castle for his room and kept on bouncing around like a ball. He did not understand how he was able to bounce and still not find his room. They all needed the lightness of the room as all were busy in grief. We all were planning a funeral for

Jacobus van Vrederic and Margriete. The town was notified as all the people wanted to come and pay their last respects to an honorable person who had fought our country till his last breath. No one actually feared the spirits as much as they loved the honorable nobleman who did not fear anything and had taken a vow to fight till the end.

Different churches had memorial services held as beautiful prayer services were held all around the small city. I realized we had to keep a distance and had to make sure we were not seen or heard by anyone. The only faces everyone had seen were Rietje and her betrothed Sir Alexander van der Bijl.

I watched Rietje handle everything so lovingly until she had fainted on top of Jacobus van Vrederic's grave surrounded with forget-me-nots. She cried screaming her lungs out as she said, "Opa please take me with you. I am worried who will rub Oma's temple if she is in pain? Also who will rub your feet when you are in pain? I can't live without you two! Please take me along! Opa I am scared to be alone."

I cried within myself in silence as I did not want anyone to see my inner soul was breaking up for my granddaughter. Margriete and Jacobus had been laid to rest next to one another as that's how they lived and had wanted to be remembered throughout time.

I was shocked how I had handled everything so quietly and did not even shed a single drop of tears. I was hiding my inner feelings for the granddaughter whom I would have to leave behind. I was not worried for myself but my granddaughter who had to learn to live by herself. I had promised my mother, Katelijne, and Griet that I would be strong and not fall prey to my emotions as we had a wedding to plan. They all wanted to lighten the heavy feelings and again headed into asking Rietje how she knew Sir Alexander was the person of her dreams.

She was shy and avoided saying anything, so Katelijne asked Sir Alexander, "Okay Big Mama and I have to know how did you two fall in love?"

The knight laughed as he said, "It was dark and cold as I saw my mystical princess with her long dark brown hair walking past the bridge. She was looking into the reflecting pond, near the castle gate. I had stopped to see if she was a human or a real spirit who was roaming around the castle I was sent to protect. She fought with me and I fell on the ground under her sword near the reflecting pond. It was a beautiful starry night when Jacobus van Vrederic had confronted me very calmly with his arms folded."

He watched Rietje and said, "As I was lying on the ground under the sharp sword of the granddaughter, I could only utter the word, 'magical.' The most honorable nobleman on Earth had asked me, 'What is so magical?' I told him I saw the Lover's Lighthouse and the kissing couple in it. Yet I swear as I saw the enchanted couple in the lighthouse kissing, all I could think was, I want to marry this entranced beloved woman standing in front of me. Even if it is on my last breath, I still would marry her and make her my entranced beloved wife."

He then watched the love of his life and said, "I promise my dear with all the sorrows life could give us, I will be there standing right by you. I promise even though not every dawn will come with blessings, as you are my blessing of life, I shall try to bring as many blessings as I can into our life. I had promised Opa, Jacobus van Vrederic, I shall never let you go. In front of all the future generations I again take a vow, dear entranced beloved, I shall never let you go. Until my last breath, I shall always be there for you and with you."

The wedding of my beautiful granddaughter Rietje and her beloved knight, Sir Alexander van der Bijl, was being held at our home Kasteel Vrederic. We had sent out the invitations yet no one had arrived. The pastors from the

Protestant Church had come as did the father and nuns from the Catholic Church. Yet not a single person from the city or even neighboring cities whom this Kasteel Vrederic family members had helped throughout the years had come.

The home was decorated with forget-me-nots and simple wildflowers as to Rietje's request. Candles were burning all around as Rietje wore her Oma's wedding dress. I watched Sir Alexander too wore the same outfit I had worn during my wedding to Margriete, the love of my life.

The spirit members of the family were all there wearing borrowed clothes from Sir Alexander and Rietje. I knew there had to be someone who should walk the bride down the aisle, as the father of the Catholic Church volunteered to do so. I knew Theunis would be here as well as I would be here walking down the aisle with her. It mattered not what everyone else saw or did not see, it only mattered what was in between my granddaughter and myself.

The feeling of loneliness was taking over Kasteel Vrederic as everyone wondered how fearful would the people be that they avoided entering the home. The pastor of the Protestant Church spoke with Sir Alexander, Rietje, and Aunt Marinda, the few people he actually could see, as he said, "The rumors spread like hot fire all around the town.

True or not true matters not, for it's what one wants to believe. Also everyone or let's say some people believe Rietje is a witch just like her grandmother was. Strangely, some of the women who were rescued by the nobleman Jacobus van Vrederic even to his deathbed also think Rietje is a witch. I guess I would say it's all good as God probably wanted to protect the child from all evil minds through this misery."

We were all interrupted by sudden thunderous noises of people stomping and running from carriages. We all looked and watched out in the direction of the sounds. There were elderly gentlemen and women running into Kasteel Vrederic as if they were in an emergency rush.

I heard a very familiar voice of an elderly man whom I recognized yet could not figure out who he was. I realized Mama told us we would not recognize everyone even though we would feel like we do know them. Yet something could click the memories back. I knew I remembered almost everything from my past life yet when I was being confronted by these memories, I realized some were still missing.

He had a walking cane with him as he walked very elegantly and said, "My great-niece will not walk alone, as I will give the bride away. My precious darling baby, this old soul is still alive even though I am over a hundred years old. I still am running strong."

I watched Mama ask, "Who is he? And is he like six hundred years old or what?"

The gentleman watched Mama and said looking directly into her eyes, "Dear child, are you not of my family lineage? You should know we never tell our age as we outlive most people. Also you are a dream psychic because I am one too. You should know my dear future generation, you have come from my family bloodline."

I watched the most beautiful bride in the world run toward the newly arrived gentleman and ask, "Bertelmeeus, how did you hear? And how did you come?"

I started to laugh as even when my precious granddaughter was a little baby and had not learned to speak properly, she had always said "Bertelmeeus" laughing in joy whenever she had seen him. She still did continue, with no uncle or great-uncle but her own cute way just as she had as a child, she continued to say Bertelmeeus. I looked at him very carefully and thought by God, he still is alive and looking young too.

I felt like a mountain was lifted from my shoulders as he looked into my eyes directly and said, "There is no way your Opa would have missed your wedding as he would have arrived as a spirit to only see you. Also how did you little one think I would leave you alone when all of these family members take their leave so quickly? I will stay with you and raise your little babies as long as you have me little one. I know my God will answer my prayers. Like I told you, this great-uncle of yours shall never let you go."

He then watched our handsome knight, Sir Alexander, and said, "You promise to do good by my child? Give me your oath and honor you will never let my child be sad or upset."

I watched Sir Alexander smile and say, "I promise to never hurt her or break our wedding vows as I love her more than my own heartbeats. For my heart beats only her name. Yet I won't promise Rietje won't ever cry or be unhappy as life is uncertain. However, if she does cry or is upset, I will be by her side as I am her knight, here to love and protect her infinitely."

In front of all the people, a very old Bertelmeeus van der Berg looked at me directly and said to Sir Alexander, "Well believe me if you do break your oath, I know my Jacobus will be standing right here, watching you even from the beyond."

Sir Alexander started to laugh as he knew Bertelmeeus too could see me as he also did and said, "Just like we all know he is standing right here watching over all of us with all of his love and care for his beloved granddaughter. The noble diarist Jacobus van Vrederic will break Heaven and Earth to be with his beloved granddaughter anyhow, anyway."

It was then we saw so many women and men had entered the wedding parlor. I realized I knew all of these people somehow yet could not place my mind as to how.

Bertelmeeus told Rietje, "All of these women and men were directly and indirectly taken care of by your Opa. These were the women he had rescued from the gallows and the stakes. The women you all rescued yesterday too wanted to come, at least some of them did but feared the repercussion by their family members who left them to die in the hand of the enemy anyway. Yet my child watch how many have come, not who has not. For these people will multiply and become your family members."

We all watched a beautiful wedding take place as the beloved great-uncle of a beloved great-niece had cried and smiled at the knowledge of how much she was truly loved. Later on, I sat and had a talk with my favorite caretaker who had taken care of the sixteenth and seventeenth-century Kasteel Vrederic.

I asked him, "You can obviously see me, so do tell me how did you hear about the wedding ceremony of Rietje and Sir Alexander? Also it would help to know what you eat so I could ask Rietje to make sure your diet is exactly the same and I pray you live long enough to see my granddaughter has a couple of children. I don't want her to be lonely."

He told me, "Jacobus, do all Kasteel Vrederic family members travel back as spirits after they pass away? I guess some of us don't come back as spirits and must live long enough as you all run away as fast as you can, leaving my little Rietje all alone. What is up there that you all run so fast? I guess you won't say. I told you when she was brought to our home only a few days old, I would never let her go. Anyway, it's rumors, they spread like wildfires. I heard about our castle being haunted and about Margriete and your death and I knew it's time I must return to my home and take care of the child I raised alongside you. Did you know rumors spread faster than even wildfires? I guess it's good sometimes. Jacobus I will miss you, and I must ask you, why did you die leaving this old man? You could have exchanged seats with me you know."

I only sat there and saw the family members of the twenty-first century all listen to all of the conversation very carefully. I told him, "No, not all of the family members do stay behind as spirits as I too shall move on. I do know how fast rumors spread so we will keep this rumor of Kasteel Vrederic being haunted last a little longer. For in this rumor also is hidden the protection of my granddaughter and her future generations. Also Bertelmeeus, I miss you terribly and do wish we had more time together. Yet I love you so much. I wonder if given all the time in the world, would it still be enough or not? I love my Kasteel Vrederic and all the members inside of this home, all of them."

Bertelmeeus asked me, "So Jacobus are you and Margriete together or have you been separated in your future life? For I had a dream you could not recognize her. So if you are separated please remember she too is searching for you. I loved Margriete like my own child. I miss her too Jacobus. I know this gap I feel in my inner soul will never be filled until I too come to you and hold both of you in my arms."

I watched Papa come and sit next to me as we both watched Bertelmeeus watch Papa and say, "I hope you have become a gentleman and are taking care of my child Jacobus. If not, then I too will come like a ghost and haunt you down. I do remember your howling screams in pain, as you had missed your beloved wife. Yet I hope you have found out from my Jacobus you can't gain back anyone by removing someone from your heart. Jacobus never replaced anyone yet he taught all how you could love all of your family members and strangers in their own place."

Papa only said, "Nice to see you too Bertelmeeus, and please don't become a ghost as of yet even though you would love to come and haunt me. For please remember you are the only family member she has aside from the time traveler Marinda and her beloved Sir Alexander. I will keep your threat in my mind and wait for your arrival. Until then, do give your complete love and care to this great-granddaughter of mine. Also please say a prayer for my son whom you too consider as your own child to be able to take being separated from Margriete better than I had. Yet I will promise you I will break heavens above and Earth below to make sure my son unites with his beloved Margriete and never again gets hurt."

The nightfall came soon as we watched the loving couple settle into their new home Kasteel Vrederic. It was then we all saw in the library on top of the fireplace, a huge portrait was hanging. In the hand-drawn portrait, there was our complete family. I saw Margriete stood next to my old self as I held on to her. There next to them stood Griet and Theunis. After them stood Rietje and Sir Alexander. Then in a separate row right below were Mama and Papa and Andries. Next to them stood Antonius and Katelijne and there on the side I was standing with my arms in a fold.

I watched my brother Antonius as he nodded and said, "Actually this portrait I did with Big Papa as a wedding gift for Rietje and Sir Alexander. Big Papa painted me in as I don't do self-portraits. Also, he is my teacher."

It was then I saw Rietje run and come to me as she said, "Opa please before you leave, tell me how I should keep going on, without you?"

I tried to hug her but knew a spirit has limitations. Yet I told her, "A nail will drown if you drop it in the water, yet a ship made out of metal does not drown because it's too big. My love for you is eternal and shall never die even though this mortal body does. You keep my memories alive by writing in your journal the conclusion chapter. Retell to your children and grandchildren the love story of an Opa and his granddaughter. For remember there is no death to the love stories as all you have to do when the story ends is read it again. Share it with someone else. Keep it going my child. My dear child it is time you must write another chapter in your life. Another story shall begin. You must now live your love story with Sir Alexander. For even when everything dies, love lives on. Remember all the stories live side by side, yet new stories must begin as old ones are put aside. All of them are remembered eternally through the pages of life."

Antonius came and sat next to Rietje and told her, "My beloved grandniece remember to keep an eye on the portrait I have painted for you, with the help of your Great-Opa. I believe it is alive as the gift was given to you with the hands of your spirit future generations still yet to come. We will keep an eye out for you as you and your husband are our family ancestors. I promise I will keep an eye out for your Opa as you had kept an eye out for him."

Rietje went and tried to give Antonius an air hug as all she said is, "Opa's heart beats Rietje, yet Opa somehow is alive for only Oma. I wonder if he will be able to take the journey back without her or me to take care of him."

I watched my family as I told Rietje, "I will defeat my inner enemies as I start the battle within myself. I have my spirit family members with me as a guide. They will be with me through this journey. Just like the great knight, Sir Alexander, shall be with you as your husband from now on forth. I know you will have a family with him in the future. A family that ties you, your children, and grandchildren with me again in the future."

I again told her, "As long as you believe in the vows of a family and keep your family intact, you will always be connected with all the future generations of this home. Remember my child we shall always defeat all enemies as we just did this time. Our family members shall always be safe in this home. For eternally all the known and unknown enemies shall always be defeated by the spirits of Kasteel Vrederic."

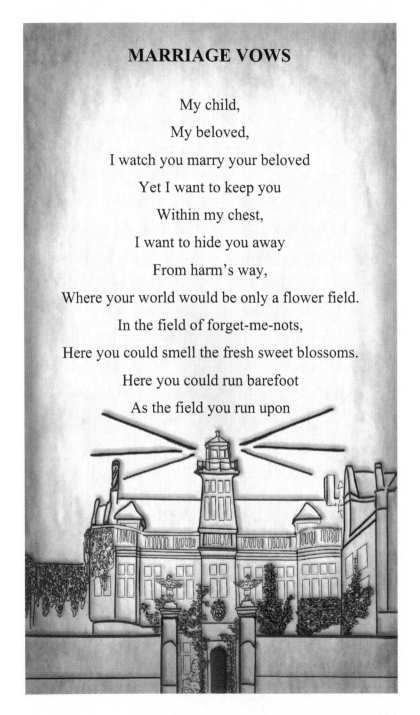

MARRIAGE VOWS

My child,

My beloved,

I watch you marry your beloved

Yet I want to keep you

Within my chest,

I want to hide you away

From harm's way,

Where your world would be only a flower field.

In the field of forget-me-nots,

Here you could smell the fresh sweet blossoms.

Here you could run barefoot

As the field you run upon

Is my chest.

The flower fields you enjoy

Are my heartbeats.

My beloved child,

Forever I have kept you hidden

Within these heartbeats.

Yet I know today even though

My heart beats your name,

I must allow another heartbeat

To keep you safe and protected within his,

As today a grandfather says to you,

Yes my granddaughter,

My heart beats your name,

As from my heart,

I shall never let you go.

Yet today,

I let you go to be safely

Within the heartbeats

Of your beloved,

As today you have

So bravely recited your

MARRIAGE VOWS.

My Beloved,

My entranced beloved granddaughter has found her entranced beloved husband on this day. I am so blessed as today through the blessed door of dreams and the tunnel of light I was able attend your sacred wedding day.

This sacred day is filled with hope and blessings and is the only path to our future generations eternally. The home you two shall share is blessed with your ancestors and is blessed with your future generations. Today as you two enter the sacred castle you shall feel all the buried love in the walls blossom around you. Today the walls of a castle too will write upon themselves another passionate romance novel.

A magical wedding day I never thought was possible yet just like a magical fairytale, it did happen. I know your Oma too was here spiritually as I stood there spiritually too. For remember upon the same walls, your Oma and I had written our passionate love story for which today we have you authoring your own story.

Remember my dear child, our family members are magical and sometimes mysterious too. Forever you shall find yourself amongst one or another family member visiting you. Just like I found out Aunt Marinda has traveled from my time period back into your time period, only to be with you.

Today for your wedding, I gift you my magical blessings as I write within the pages of your diary I carry with me. For the blank pages of your diary were filled through my ink and my pen within the pages of your diary. Remember to always believe in the powers of love and magic, and the magical bond between families. They shall never fail you.

Yes my beloved, my heart beats your name. Today you too have your diary in your hands for us to have in the future, all magically written through the magical door of dreams.

With all my love on your wedding day,

Opa

CHAPTER TEN:

Entry By Antonius Van Phillip

"Time passes by without any notice yet it leaves behind memories. These memories written within the pages of a diary become immortal even beyond human lives which are sadly mortal."

Dr. Jacobus Vrederic van Phillip crosses time leaving his beloved wife of the sixteenth century behind, only to find her waiting for him in the twenty-first century, yet will he recognize her? Maybe a baby who travels with bread could help him?

L ife is a miracle in itself. Yet there are some people around us who make living through life a miracle and a blessing. I am Antonius van Phillip, and I will be entering this part of our journey within the pages of my grandniece's diary as promises made are only true when promises are kept.

Today I have taken my brother Jacobus Vrederic van Phillip's given oath to his granddaughter as my responsibility and I will finish his journey through my pen. This is our family oath as we call this our vows from the beyond. However, we were all on a journey to meet and greet the authors of the *I Shall Never Let You Go* diarists, when we realized our family ancestors were in trouble and so forth our complete family tree was in jeopardy if we didn't intercede so be it miraculously. We had to break the door of the unknown in order to save our family dynasty.

A blessed wedding ceremony was held for my grandniece, Margriete "Rietje" Jacobus van Peters, and her twin flame, a real-life knight, Sir Alexander van der Bijl. Margriete wanted Rietje to wear her wedding dress and had saved it for her. Somehow Margriete had arranged all the wedding supplies and gown and even the flowers before her death. I know Margriete wanted to be here with the sixteenth-century Jacobus van Vrederic to give Rietje away.

It was a somber day as I watched Rietje's tears retelling her feelings throughout the day. Rietje's heartfelt sorrows and love all in one were also visible in my twenty-first-century brother's eyes. He held Rietje's glances with his own eyes and reassured her he was there, be it spiritually. He was present at her wedding and that was a blessing given to both of them from above.

After the blessed wedding, we had to quickly bid our parting to all the family members of the seventeenth-century Kasteel Vrederic family. I watched my brave brother hang in there throughout the complete journey. I knew he had wished with all his heart Margriete, his twin flame, could have been there. I too prayed for the hundredth time if only she could have awakened from under the ground where she was buried in the seventeenth century with her husband of the same time period, my big brother's past incarnated form.

I wished Margriete could have just walked out of the grave and stood next to my big brother. I knew this prayer was taking a lot of time to be answered. Yet somehow I knew Margriete was up and walking about yet in the twenty-first century, where we too must be heading back.

We all had avoided the garden of *EVERMORE BELOVED* where there were two newly laid graves. Our family's favorite forget-me-nots were planted all around the gravesite. We had asked Jacobus not to go and visit his own grave from his previous life as he had seen it in the future many times over. I wanted him to not get in a bond with his twin flame, which in my mind was feasible, yet I was worried how feasible it was knowing my brother. I shivered in fear.

As the sun was setting on the river near the gravesite, we returned to the ground next to the Kasteel Vrederic library where from we had come and landed upon. The main house was not far from the gravesite of the Kasteel Vrederic family members. The amazing sky above us was sitting with her art canvas as he was painting an amazing picture. A calm and sorrow-filled artwork where no one spoke or said anything. Yet it felt like the nightingales were all out trying to sing some sad songs of separation, and maybe promises of until we meet again. Within the imagination of an artist, I kept this scenario to paint later after our return.

My brother Jacobus Vrederic van Phillip had taken a shower. How though I did not ask, as my brother would not change his daily shower habits, even though we were all dream traveling through the seventeenth century. I saw his brown hair was dripping cold water around his broad shoulders. His brown eyes were lost in his own world.

My brother's height and my height are exactly the same, we both are six feet tall. Shorter than Big Papa yet Big Mama was happy she could reach us faster than Big Papa. I so much wanted to be cool like my big brother. I had grown my French beard to match his. Yet today I worried for my brother more than I imagined a person could even worry and still be alive to write in a journal. I realized my hands were shaking in fear of what was laying ahead of me.

I saw Big Papa had come near me and he held my hands in his and said in my ears, "I am here, we shall cross this together."

After the sun set in the amazing sky above us, we walked to the gravesite of our ancestors. Big Mama and Big Papa watched Jacobus while everyone was thinking as to what his plans were for this time. I watched my brave Big Mama too was shaking like myself. I held on to her hands as I watched her try to steady herself.

Big Mama said, "Remember boys, we must return soon or we shall all be stuck in a no man's land forever. I feel strange as if someone is calling us and wants to wake us up yet we are not responding. So come on, let's finish the visit quickly and return together. If one of us stays behind, he or she will remain here forever and the others will wake up but won't be able to awaken him or her. Please everyone listen to me, we must return like now."

Jacobus was silent as if he could not hear anything and just watched Margriete's gravesite. He was refusing to move from her gravesite whilst he kept on watching the skies above our head. There were signs of rainstorms approaching us while Big Mama rushed and said we must all move quickly. She called the spirits Theunis and Griet.

She said, "My beloved grandchildren, would you two start your magical touch and place us to sleep?"

Griet said, "Oma I am worried for Papa as he looks different. Even though I have not been lucky enough to see him while I was living, I actually have known him for eternity, as it seems. Also I love him eternally."

Then as the skies roared signaling of thunder and rain, Jacobus screamed and fell on top of Margriete's gravesite saying, "Oh my God no, my darling will be scared. Margriete don't be scared my beloved. I won't leave you alone. I will cover you from the rain with my own body eternally I promise. Sleep peacefully my love as I will lay on top of you as I know my body also lays by your side. In all my forms, I shall be by your side."

He looked up at Mama and said, "She was on top of me the first time I saw her Mama. She was trying to heal me from a horrible cold and fell asleep on my chest. She stayed with me while even Papa left me as he lost his mind by losing you. How could I leave her behind while she lies asleep in the cold wet grounds? I know she is scared of this storm. I am my father's son and now I do understand why he had lost his mind. Because you left him as you had burned to ashes, he became a living walking vessel which held your memories."

Then he got up and looked at the skies and shouted, "Dear skies don't you see my beloved is asleep? Listen to a crazy lover and his calls! For Heaven's sake, please stop this musical drama she does not enjoy but is scared of. I know you are powerful and huge so you scare off little people, like her. Please don't you see? She is so small and powerless and she is scared of these storms. Also if you are listening then do leave a cloud over her during the days when the sun is out trying to burn down my Margriete for she burns quickly. Also stop pouring on her for she catches a cold very quickly and she will never complain about herself to anyone."

I watched my brother fall on her grave and say, "Dear Lord, I have failed her, for how was it she had healed me during our first encounter and today I leave her here in the cold grounds? I, a doctor of the twenty-first century, could not even heal her."

I saw him then kiss her grave and say, "Dear gorgeous one, don't be frightened if the moon is not out for she has confessed to me, you are so beautiful she wants you to shine not her. She too loves you just like all others. Also if the sun refuses to shine, it's because he too loves you too much and wants to protect you not burn you. Sleep peacefully my love and the beholder of my life as I will always be here next to you."

I watched my brother faint on top of Margriete's gravesite as Big Mama and Big Papa screamed in fear. They both broke out in cries and asked the Lord, "Please be merciful! Lord be merciful! We beg you not to give any more pain to a man who physically and emotionally only healed all around him."

I knew I had asked Sir Alexander to keep Rietje inside Kasteel Vrederic and wait for the diaries to send back entries as we did not want anything to go wrong. We feared Rietje would not be able to take the separation of being left alone. She would have broken down seeing her Opa in this situation. Also Mama said only the people who had come with us were allowed to go back with us as this was still all a dream we must wake up from.

I watched our brave soldier Theunis and his wife try to lift Jacobus but could not as they were still somehow spirits and we were all becoming humans. Griet cried for her beloved father and her beloved mother as it was hard for her to be in this situation. I wanted to hug her and knew this was the only time I could hug her until we get her back as my blessed niece.

I hugged both of them as I heard Theunis screamed and said, "Quickly before all of you turn into human dust, I must put you to sleep so you can walk through the tunnel of light back to your home."

I watched Big Mama cry and say, "I can't keep on losing my sons, I can't take any more loss. Erasmus help please. My boys keep on wandering off as they please. Katelijne, my daughter, please don't let go of my Andries. Antonius, you and Jacobus hold on to one another. Erasmus come on, bring back my sons to me now!"

I knew what I had to do as I watched my son Andries watch me from Katelijne's lap. I realized the urgency is now and I will not lose one more of my family members. Death loves my family members as the saying in my family goes, there must be a very good holiday home up in Heaven that my family members get free vacation time in, that they run off to even without saying their goodbyes.

I told Big Mama and Big Papa, "Everyone, I promise all of you I will not allow any members of my family to die.

I lost my parents and was blessed with Big Mama and Big Papa. Yet I realized I was meant to be Big Mama and Big Papa's son, for I would not replace my Big Mama, my mother anywhere or anytime. I lost my twin brother and miraculously I have him back as my son. Today I will not lose my big brother, so with or without your permission I shall carry you back Jacobus. Once you do get to read Rietje's diary, I know you will probably scream at me. However hey big bro, I love you more than I love my own life."

Big Papa and Big Mama with tears nodded giving me permission to carry my big brother, so I lifted my brother up like a child over my shoulder and walked back to the spot we all had arrived at through the tunnel of light. I started to laugh as I always break out in laughter while I am scared and I said, "Big bro you are heavy, yet I love you too much to dump you anywhere. So here we go, let's begin this run. I will walk fast you guys, I have a heavy one."

Big Mama watched me and said, "Antonius don't be scared. Mama is here, you can do it."

I knew to this day my mother sees what I am thinking even without any words being uttered. It's all in her eyes, the way she looks at me or even before my sight, the way she would grab my hands I knew the woman saw everything inside and out. She had told us as a child she could see us inside and out. I started to laugh again and stopped as I had big bro on my shoulders, and I certainly didn't want to drop my big brother.

Before we began our return journey, I watched Big Papa go and sit next to Margriete and his previous life's incarnated son's grave and say, "Forever I have loved you my son. Maybe I could not express my feelings as somehow I was able to hide my emotions better than ever expressing them. I had kept my feelings hidden and I hurt myself as well as you. Yet never would I change the way you turned out to be my noble son. Also Margriete, I promise I will find you and not go off on any holidays up there, until I bring you and Griet and our beloved Rietje back home, to Kasteel Vrederic, so help me God."

Then the spirits of Kasteel Vrederic touched me first and then all of my family members on our forehead as we then found ourselves walking through the tunnel of light. We ran and entered the tunnel of light as we fell asleep and woke up and saw ourselves walking in a tunnel. A dizzying spell came over my entire body as I heard a voice say in the tunnel, "Everyone must walk on their own through this tunnel, as they came alone unless a minor who shall be accompanied by an angel."

I watched my family members and told the voice, "Make me walk alone if you so will. For I shall not leave my big brother here alone. He carried all of my troubles on his shoulders all alone and now I must do the same for him. Why is it we are allowed to help and guide one another on Earth and in the tunnel we must walk alone? Then I ask an angel to help my brother walk back home with me. He is a minor right now as he can't walk for himself. I had no vision as I had entered Earth, and it was there even as an adult my big brother drove me everywhere as I was not allowed to drive. I guess I was a minor."

It was then I heard Katelijne say, "I don't know who you are but if you are God then know this man was not even related to me but had saved my life without even thinking about it twice. He walked with me and had taken care of all my costs without being related by blood. I accepted him as my brother in this life and eternally. Forever I shall be by his side with my husband as even for me I love my big brother more than I love my own life. I shall intercede for him and I ask you to please allow us to take him back."

I watched the spirits of our castle walk with us as Theunis said, "I know for certain Jacobus has gone out of his way to even save my bride and me even when he did not know I was his son-in-law. He helped all the known and unknown women and men in his other life as well as this one. Forever I have followed him like a shadow. Everyone on this Earth knows us as the spirits of Kasteel Vrederic yet we are the guiding angels of Jacobus in all of his forms."

Griet our very quiet and shy child said, "Papa has been blamed for not even knowing of a child he had, yet he searched for me throughout my life. It's not his nor my fault but my Lord, you did not give me enough time to even get to know my father or my child. Today as we walk through the tunnel, Kasteel Vrederic will have my daughter and her beloved husband guiding all lost lovers back together again until she too is reborn and can hand over this job to yet another. Yet today I ask you my Lord to allow my father to be saved as it is you who had given him the honor to be known as a great nobleman. So today please allow another miracle to take place for a man who has been loved by even his enemies."

Big Mama watched the light and said, "Jacobus is the only nobleman who will do for all whatever they need. He will help all and save them with his medical knowledge if he can. My Lord, why do we need to tell you of all the deeds that are already known to you? Within my knowledge, it is said you too keep a diary of all humans' deeds. So my Creator, today why not go through his deeds and let all the prayers given to him by the unknown strangers he had saved save him too?"

Big Papa came and placed his hands on my shoulders and said, "If anyone must be left behind, then I, the father, of this son shall volunteer but spare my son please."

Big Mama ran and held Big Papa and said, "How dare you volunteer without me! Who do you think you are? What do you think of yourself? Don't you know I too can't live without you or my children? Anyway, don't you dare repeat those words as I will scream and ruin all of your eardrums and all of those who are walking through here too."

I watched my young baby boy sleep in his mother's arms so peacefully. He called his mother "woman" as he called Big Mama "mother." I knew he was my brother's incarnation. I then told my family members, "Calm down everyone. We will all go home safely as I know I will be able to take my brother back home to the twenty-first-century Kasteel Vrederic safely. A vow I had taken I will complete."

It was a never-ending journey as we reached a door which said the door of death. Big Mama walked past it as we all followed her. Then we saw a door which had said the door of judgment. We all again followed Big Mama and walked past it. Then we came to a door which said the Omnipotent.

Big Mama said, "It's not time yet even though I would love to enter this door. However, we must keep on going. The door we shall arrive at next is where I want Griet and Theunis to enter. Remember to stay together and here you go, I have a ribbon in my hands for you two. As you see the Ferris wheel, do get on it and do not let go of one another. I will keep on praying to be able to see you both on the other side. Remember your parents have been born Griet, so very soon you too shall arrive. Do not be scared."

We all saw the brave couple, the spirits of Kasteel Vrederic after centuries of being just spirits finally and so ever bravely walk into the tunnel of reincarnation. I was scared for them and for Rietje.

Big Mama knew and said, "Rietje will still see them as the time difference remember is a lot. So even though we are thinking we had left Rietje back home just now, actually because of the time difference, she won't miss her parents as they will be entering the reincarnation tunnel just now. So, actually now it's time my son must find his twin flame and have Griet soon."

I laughed to myself as I was carrying my brother over my shoulder. I thought big bro get over this obstacle quickly as Big Mama is planning for your wedding in her mind. I can see it and know she probably is window shopping in her mind.

I only heard Katelijne say, "Big Mama can we start shopping for big brother's wedding as these things do take time?"

I saw Big Mama only laugh and hug Katelijne. I was worried why we were not at the door yet as our door should have found us by now. I knew Big Mama too was worried why the door did not come to us yet as she kept on looking in different directions.

Big Papa asked, "Sweetheart, are we lost? Why does it seem longer? The return journey somehow is taking more time than our journey to the seventeenth century."

Big Mama said, "No, not really, but we do need someone to awaken us as we are all asleep right now. We really need a close family member to come to the library and wake us up somehow. I know Nani and Grandmother won't disturb us even if they find us all sleeping on the floor of the library. Yet I remember all of us had left the home together and no one was left behind. So I am a little worried who will awaken our bodies. We might all have sleep paralysis as we will hear people and won't be able to move or awaken until someone close to us touches us."

I realized what was going on yet the doctor with us was unconscious and we all had no idea what to do. So we remained quiet and thought some kind of miracle must happen for us to find a helping hand who would wake us up.

So I asked Big Mama, "Can you hear anything or see anything as you are the dream psychic Big Mama. I thought it said on Google during sleep paralysis if we try to move ourselves or try to make sounds, we can wake up."

She said, "You Googled Antonius? Well, I will ask you why you Googled later. Yes, I see someone has entered our Kasteel Vrederic. She is watching the Lover's Lighthouse and she sees something in it. She is trying to read what it says yet her glasses are missing or she has lost them or something."

I asked Big Mama what else do you see as she said, "I can see there is a tall man with her who said he is worried why Kasteel Vrederic is empty. He has a key somewhere but somehow lost it. I can see the woman asked him is it in his handbag. He told her, yes he thinks so. He was calling for someone. I can barely hear him yet I think he just said, 'Erasmus.' Now he is saying he is your brother Matthias and he is finally back home, after his years of traveling through India."

That's when Big Papa said, "What? Matthias is back after all of these years? You know him Anadhi. Remember he is one of my two cousins yet we consider ourselves brothers. Antonius and Andries's father was the one who had passed away so we adopted our two boys. Yet Matthias never married and had settled in India. I wonder why he finally came back. I am so happy though to have my brother back home again."

That's when Big Papa said, "Anadhi sweetheart you sleep talk all the time remember. It really does not bother me as I love you more than all of your sleep talking. So why not start to sleep talk loudly because you usually wake up the whole house with your sleep talking."

I watched Big Mama and said, "Big Mama your sleep talking is naturally loud and wakes up the whole house. We never needed an alarm to wake up for school as you sleep talked and had awakened all of us. Please my beloved mother, now start talking and maybe someone will hear you."

Then I saw my baby boy and told Big Mama, "Big Mama, Andries sleep talks like you. Maybe you two can talk now and your sounds will reach their ears. Usually if one of you starts talking, the other one does. We wondered how you slept with Andries on your chest. While he talks in his sleep, you answer him from your sleep."

Big Mama looked at all of us upset and said, "I don't know if I really sleep talk or not, as I don't hear myself. It's only what you all say. Also I am a mother and I had to keep an eye out for my boys even while I slept."

We all watched Big Mama and said in union, "You do sleep talk."

That's when baby Andries woke up and jumped into Big Mama's arms and said with a shriek, "Big Mama tell woman Andries does not want to sleep. Tell woman now!"

Then Andries watched Katelijne and said, "Woman no sleep okay. I will not sleep okay. Woman did you hear me, no sleep okay."

Big Mama copied Andries and said a little differently, "Woman no sleep okay! We will not sleep!"

That's when my baby boy started to cry even louder. We all heard voices near us. A warm hand touched me and I woke up first. I saw Jacobus was still in my arms sleeping throughout the journey. I walked over to all of my family members and woke them up one by one.

Big Mama woke up and said, "We are all back home again. Jacobus wake up my son. What is wrong with you?

Wake up. Don't you dare disobey me or I will come to where you are and wake you up over there."

Big Papa started to scream as he asked, "Antonius why is your brother not waking up? What is wrong with him?"

We all saw Uncle Matthias, as Big Papa tried to update him on all that had happened to us over one night of being missing from this world yet we were there for days. It did feel like we had lived another life over there.

That's when we saw an Indian-looking woman standing in our library. We all asked her who she was as Uncle Matthias tried to introduce her to us. We knew we were being rude as we were all nervous and worried about Jacobus and his physical state.

Uncle Matthias said, "She has accompanied me back home as I was not well. She is originally from the Netherlands. We met in New Delhi, India as she was visiting her family members over there. She lives in Scheveningen overlooking the North Sea in The Hague, South Holland. She helped me on the return flight as I was not well and actually became very ill from Dengue fever. This young woman had volunteered to help me throughout my return flight. In the airplane, I had fainted and they called and asked if there was any doctor on board. She volunteered."

I told him, "Well our doctor is unwell at home otherwise he could have checked you. We will take you in for a checkup as soon as we can figure out what is wrong with Jacobus."

That's when the woman standing near us talked and said, "What? Did I hear you right? You said his name is Jacobus? Is this the Vrederic House? I mean Kasteel Vrederic? I am a doctor. I am known as Margriete van Achthoven, and I am a cardiologist. I have my own clinic here in Amsterdam, North Holland. If you would want me to take a look at your son, I would be more than happy to."

My family members were all numb at her sight. Without any warnings we all watched her as she probably thought we were the rudest family in the world. Yet as she was speaking, I thought I saw baby Rietje was standing next to her. I promise I saw the child had a huge piece of bread in her hands.

Margriete watched us and said, "I am half Indian as my mother is Indian and my father is Dutch. I wonder is it that I am Indian that makes all of you fear me that you all are staring at me?"

Big Mama came to her senses first as she said, "No we were all having sleep paralysis and it is taking us some time to speak properly. I am also half Indian and it's my honor to meet someone like myself. Also if you don't mind me asking you said your name is Margriete? And why is baby Rietje standing next to you?"

She watched all of us and said, "Please I think all of you are having some kind of hallucination or something. I have heard rumors of spirits in Kasteel Vrederic. I must let you know I am very single and have no intention of having a child out of wedlock."

She watched us for a while and then said, "Please let me see him, I don't know why I feel like I must take care of him first. Maybe then I can answer all of your questions. I really need to go home as I only wanted your family member to reach his house safely. I had a strange premonition I must take him to his home as someone over there was calling me."

It was so weird as my whole family said at once, "Margriete, we were calling you. All of us, we were waiting for you."

She passed us and went to Jacobus and watched him sleep so peacefully on the couch. She said nothing but just watched him. I promise I saw tears fall from her eyes as she just watched him. She then touched him to check his pulse, as Jacobus jumped up and grabbed the petite Margriete by her hands and placed her on his chest and said, "Margriete don't leave me."

Margriete tried to slap him and said, "How dare you place me in your chest! Also why are you asking me not to leave? And your family is scaring me by saying they have been waiting for me."

That's when Jacobus said, "Who are you and why have you been sleeping on my chest? By God, women these days don't spare a moment and just jump on top of anyone they see."

She then did slap him and said, "I am Margriete and you grabbed me. I did not sleep on top of you, ask your family members."

Big Papa said, "Son, you deserved the slap. She did not get on top of you, but it was you who pulled her on top of you. Also Jacobus, I really don't mind, she just might be a good bride for you."

It was then Jacobus said, "You are no Margriete as I would know her anywhere, anytime."

Margriete screamed and said, "I am Margriete as my parents named me Margriete and how dare you tell me I am not me but someone else. You are having an identity crisis, not me."

Jacobus then said, "You don't have any parents as you were an orphan, remember?"

Margriete looked at Big Papa and said, "You look like a normal person. Please take this man to a psychiatrist as he needs one. I can't help him as I am a cardiologist. I work with hearts and obviously this man has none. Yet he needs to have his head examined."

Big Papa embarrassed our family even more as he ran after Margriete when she was leaving. He said, "My dear child please don't leave as we must get you married to our son and have your child, so we can say dear forbidden daughter of Kasteel Vrederic, I shall never let you go."

Margriete watched Big Papa and told Big Mama, "Please take him with you to the doctor as it seems like both father and son need help. I am worried for him too."

After this, she left our home. Our family members were all jumping up and down in joy as Margriete came to us and we never had to even leave Kasteel Vrederic. Jacobus, however, was furious with Big Papa and Big Mama and all of us for trying to get him attached to a woman who just had Margriete's name.

Yet as she was leaving, she did say, "Jacobus I told you, you won't recognize me even though you had said, anywhere, anytime."

Then I watched my Big Papa say, "Actually I had said anywhere, anytime. My son just takes after his father. You see you actually have something that belongs to us."

Margriete left in a rush as Big Papa kept on saying even after she left, "Anadhi, she has my granddaughter with her. How dare she walk away when we only want what belongs to us."

Big Mama said, "I know Erasmus, but the way you are talking people will say you both need a doctor. Also I must start planning for a wedding. I don't have time for these odd things. Katelijne come my daughter. I must now start searching for your sister, my other daughter, Jacobus's bride for in this house, we don't have daughters-in-law but only daughters."

I do hope my grandniece reads this part of the entry in her diary. For my dear grandniece, it seems like we are almost ready to welcome your Oma back to our home. I know you will find this diary as a keepsake as this will even take you to the future.

If you ever need anything, remember to just open your own diary and read all the entries. If there are any updates, we will let you know. Please do keep an eye out for the next diary, as I hope your Opa writes again his love story from the twenty-first century. Big Papa is already calling it,

Forbidden Daughter Of Kasteel Vrederic: Vows From The Beyond.

With love and blessings to you and your husband, remember my beloved grandniece you are forever your Great-Opa's, Great-Oma's, Opa's, I know your Oma's, your grandaunt's, and my entranced beloved, we shall never let you go.

Entry by,

Antonius van Phillip

SWEET DARLING RIETJE

Falling in love

Means you invite sorrows.

This game of love

Is made out of tears.

When you fall in love, you are there.

Yet when we become separated,

Love still lives

Through memories,

Through pain and sorrow

Of being separated.

Love only grows old.

Even though humans

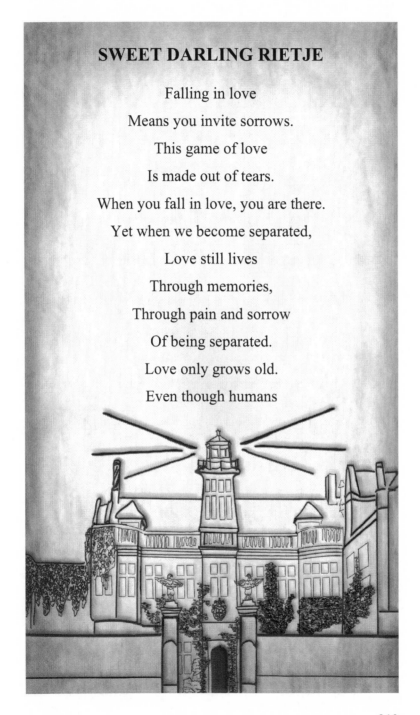

Depart this Earth,

Love lives on eternally.

Through the bond

Of a beloved child

And her beloved family members,

The bond becomes immortal

Just like your love and our love

In union has created our family,

The family of Kasteel Vrederic,

Where you and all of us

Live within the same walls,

Yet in different time periods.

Yet remember my sweet child,

Just feel us over there

As we feel you over here.

Through our home,

Our Kasteel Vrederic,

We shall always be there for you, our

SWEET DARLING RIETJE.

Dear Rietje,

Today I actually saw you here as a baby, standing next to Margriete. I have complete faith in all of our visions and above all I have complete faith in our home, the blessed Kasteel Vrederic, where dreams do come true. Remember to keep the door of dreams open to your faith and belief. For through this magical door, you too shall travel all around the world and even through time. Eternally my love and blessings be with you. Until we meet again.

Your granduncle,

Antonius van Phillip

CONCLUSION

Kasteel Vrederic Family Tree

"I have planted a seed and I watch it grow, for I know the tree that I have planted today shall grow and produce more trees even beyond my time."

Margriete "Rietje" Jacobus Peters, as an elderly woman, sits at the EVERMORE BELOVED garden and remembers her Opa, cherishing the memories of a granddaughter's blessed journey with her beloved granddfather.

I am Rietje and this is the conclusion chapter of my diary. Today we had a very sunny day here at Kasteel Vrederic. A warm and cozy morning where I still at this age have my fresh baked bread in my hands as bread still appears like a miracle. I have always loved to visit the *EVERMORE BELOVED* garden of Kasteel Vrederic as it had gotten rid of my fears of death, for how wonderful it would be to just be here with my family members.

I love to sit on the bench Opa and I had made when I was a small child. My husband Sir Alexander, my knight, had come into my life as my conqueror and never let me go as he promised he would hold on to me until his last breath. I sat here in his arms so many times as it seems like a lifetime.

I do have dreams though as if soon I too will join my family members in this miraculous garden when it is my time I understand. The forget-me-nots and the wildflowers have grown here meticulously. All the fruit trees planted around the garden give shade and fruits to all who visit.

I have had a blessed journey through my life. As an orphan, I had lost my parents to the Dutch Eighty Years' War. Yet I was blessed as with every tragedy there is some kind of a hidden gift, if you only can find it. I did, I found my Opa after becoming an orphan.

I was raised by my Opa all by himself until Oma had arrived. I was there to save my Oma from being burned at the stakes with my Opa during the unjust witch burnings, which had spread throughout Europe and I hear even in the Americas. After this event, we had peace in our home, Kasteel Vrederic, for a long period of time as I too was weighed as a child at the blessed witches' weighing house in Oudewater.

Yet as time would bring grief upon our hands, the seventeenth century had brought upon my life a lot of grief. First I found my entranced beloved knight like a tale Oma and Opa had read to me over the years as he arrived in my life. He had come as the heaven-sent glow of sunshine within my life. Yet little did I know the biggest storm of my life would be arriving soon.

Yes after the glowing light of hope, our castle was taken over by the Spanish army as revenge against my honorable Opa for saving us from being burned or hung as witches. The storm proved to be the worst period of my life. Yet this storm also came with a huge miracle, as I found my future generations accompanying me during this period only through a miracle. My spirit parents brought from the future, my own future lineage. My Opa too came back to only bury himself and his beloved love of his life, his evermore beloved, my Oma.

I don't know how he took the whole situation then, yet I know it was extremely painful and had internally ripped him from inside out. I only wished I could have done something or been there for him as he was always there for me. I watched my Opa leave me alone for the second time as he left like he came, in a fog. One Opa left me and fell asleep and the other one left like a mist.

However, my Great-Oma had left me with a gift. As a dream psychic, she gave me the gift of dreams. I had been traveling time to the future through dreams. I can actually see my family either being happy or at times they would get into trouble where I tried to communicate with them.

I got busy with life as I had given birth to our triplets. Three daughters who don't look alike and actually are so different from one another. My beloved husband Alexander and I gave our castle to all three equally divided, yet the girls gave it to their oldest sister, older by a minute. We call her Anadhi after Great-Oma, yet everyone has asked me how I knew her name as it was not mentioned anywhere else. I had told all, in my dream. The other two are named Margriete and Griet.

I am so blessed as I have planted my seeds and I know our family tree will continue to grow. From this tree, my Opa will again be reborn and I hope Mama finds a blessed home this time with Oma and Opa. Did you know I had stayed awake worrying about what had happened to my family in the future? Then I was gifted with my dreams.

The diary did come back all filled up with the details about how Opa had traveled time to see and save me. Alexander and I had kept the sanctified diary filled up through the pure hands of my Opa and granduncle, as our guidance throughout life. I remember as a child, Opa had told me he would rip the skies apart to come and be with me. Also whenever I had needed him in life, he arrived not only in a spirit form but also in my dreams. Never was I actually left alone as I had the diary to guide me whenever I needed guidance.

Alexander, my knight in shining armor, had always kept me within his chest, never too far away yet always close to him. He made sure when my tears would fall, he would be there to wipe them away. He and I were gifted with a blessed family as we had little feet running across Kasteel Vrederic always asking about the portrait Granduncle Antonius had painted with Great-Opa before they left. I told my family members this was the biggest gift I hold on to as it made my faith ever stronger in my magical home.

Today I have buried my husband, my blessed knight, as old age had him leave me and go ahead of me on his journey through the tunnel of light. I have buried him here, in the same garden I had buried Opa and Oma, and Mama and Papa. My three daughters and their children, my grandchildren, are all here with me. I don't feel lonely as I have all of them during the daylight hours and my dreams during the cold nights.

There in my dreams, now I also see my dear husband who too is a star glowing in the skies above my head and I am assuming your head too. Opa, please hug Great-Oma for me, as she somehow blessed me with the presence of my spirit parents throughout my lifetime. Yet I understand reading the diary, they have journeyed through the reincarnation door. I know now I too have hope of meeting you one more time. Actually now I feel like my diary too is complete as I know my parents are traveling to be with you all again.

Opa, I can feel you in the library near the fireplace when I sit in the library. I know you somehow are there. I sometimes can see people walk around the house. As you know the rumors still are going around the city, our home

Kasteel Vrederic is haunted. Yet it has given me comfort as I know our home is safeguarded by my family members. I say to everyone our home is not haunted but safeguarded by my family members across the periods of time. For how could all who ask to be guided to their beloved twin flames still get their wishes granted, if this home was not a sacred and blessed home? For do you know Opa, people from near and far still come and wish for their beloved in front of the Lover's Lighthouse?

I only wait for my time to become a star and maybe then I too could travel time and be with my beloved Opa. Yet I wanted to give you a message from my time period that your beloved Rietje did have a blessed life, always wrapped within my home's spiritual guidance. Also the fresh baked bread always kept all of us in a happy mood as we made a tradition to always break our bread during all meals.

However, Opa I had a dream where Oma was very different and the only obstacle in uniting you two was your ability to not recognize her as she has changed her costume. Don't fall in love with her in a way that you don't recognize her for herself. I only pray if she is in front of you, do recognize her beyond the cover.

Don't let her slip away only because you don't see her beyond the cover. I wish I could have told you more as that's all I saw in my dreams. I know Great-Oma is with you, and she can guide you toward your destiny.

Granduncle Antonius, I hope maybe sometime soon I too can be with you and Andries. If not physically, I will always be there spiritually. Thank you my dear granduncle for placing your entry into my diary as it completes the book.

Opa, the diary actually was delayed in transportation. However, my blessed dreams have kept me traveling time to your time period. I know the ships coming back from India also get delayed. Some get lost in the wild sea. Yet I found each chapter in my diary being completed slowly and completely filled and returned exactly seven days after you all had left me. It was a blessed day and a blessed gift for Alexander and me. I had sent you letters throughout the years which I hope reached you safely. I wanted to send you back the completed conclusion chapter of my diary today. For Opa today, I have turned one hundred years old. I hope to celebrate this blessed day with my whole family in my favorite garden, *EVERMORE BELOVED*, the garden Opa and I had started together.

Opa, in 1648, we finally found independence. I felt somehow strange as I really wished you could have seen this day. You had fought so hard to get independence for our small country. Yet even though you could not see it physically, I know you can see it and feel it through my eyes.

Also Opa, I had done one thing without your permission, as I had allowed my great-uncle, Bertelmeeus, to be buried here in the *EVERMORE BELOVED* garden. It was his only wish as he passed away after raising my three daughters. He lived a blessed life as I saw how much he had loved my three daughters. Even my three daughters' first word was Bertelmeeus. He had said that made his life a blessed journey. He only wished you could have been here to bury him, not the other way around.

He said he too wants to be reborn around you in all of his next incarnations if it is his destiny to be reborn on Earth. If not then he wants to sleep near you as he said you are the son he never had yet did have all of his life. I actually felt good my Bertelmeeus too stayed near me all of his life and now even from the beyond. He had taken care of me as a child, yet I had taken care of him during his last days.

I hope Opa you too found Oma back in your life. If not, then I would ask Great-Opa to intercede. Remember Great-Opa, if you and Great-Oma do recognize Oma, then don't let Opa and Oma be separated at any cost.

My blessings be with my family forever. May this home always find everlasting love stories throughout time and tide. Also dear family of the twenty-first century please know, like my blessed husband, you all are and shall always be my,

ENTRANCED BELOVED: I SHALL NEVER LET YOU GO

Signed,

Margriete "Rietje" Jacobus Peters

P.S. I know Opa's heart beats Rietje, yet my heart too forever beats only for Opa. I hope the elixir serum Alexander and I had poured over our family tree is always full of newly grown green leaves since this tree is our Kasteel Vrederic family tree.

KASTEEL VREDERIC FAMILY TREE

I am part of the tree

That you my family had planted.

With your hands,

You sowed me upon your tree.

I grew from young to become an old leaf

On the same tree.

I nourished and watched the tree grow

When it was my time to take care of it.

Throughout time,

Some leaves have fallen off our tree.

As you too had left me swinging

In the air all alone,

When you had fallen off of the tree.

Yet through time,

I watched new leaves grow back on the tree,

Which gave me company.

I watched the tree lose so many leaves

In front of my eyes,

As I had nothing I could do

But water it with my pouring tears.

I also watched the newly released buds

Come in with smiling sunshine and new leaves.

Yet I wonder

When will I fall off this tree,

As I am now an old orange leaf

Ready to fall off.

I hope maybe

Then I too could join all of you,

The ones who have left me to be all alone.

I could then perhaps again

Dance, sing, be happy,

And twirl in the happy breeze of joy,

As I had once upon a time

Orbited next to you all.

So I wait to be once again

A new grown leaf in the

KASTEEL VREDERIC FAMILY TREE.

Dear Opa,

Please know I have planted a family tree for you. If life could give me a second chance, I would only want Mama, Papa, Great-Opa, Great-Oma, Granduncle Antonius, Grandaunt Katelijne, Uncle Andries, and my beloved Opa and Oma to raise me in the Kasteel Vrederic all over again. Yes Bertelmeeus too must be around us as how could Kasteel Vrederic be without him?

I would also pray that I always have my twin flame Sir Alexander van der Bijl to be my husband forever. He was my strength while I felt weakened by the loss of my family members, especially you Opa. He also reminded me every single day how the moon glows when I smiled and the sun stayed behind the clouds as I cried. He made me laugh and we cried together during the sorrows of our life. Yet I pray today may I be with him eternally as he is my entranced beloved husband.

I hope may our family always be happy and keep on writing eternal, evermore, and entranced beloved love stories throughout time. Opa I had wished upon the stars each night, may our stories cross over to be our vows from the beyond. For here we all say, I shall never let you go. And we all hope to join the diaries of *Vows From The Beyond.*

Forever my love shall blossom within your heartbeats Opa, for this granddaughter shall forever say to you, my dear Opa, my entranced beloved Opa, the spirit Opa that came to my wedding, I shall never let you go. If only you were mine, I would have held on to you forever. Yet I want you to find Oma quickly and then I know again I too will say to both of you from my heartbeats, I shall never let you go.

This is my diary and I am,

Margriete "Rietje" Jacobus Peters

THE INHABITANTS OF ENTRANCED BELOVED

Dr. Jacobus Vrederic van Phillip
Son of Erasmus van Phillip and Anadhi Newhouse van Phillip, cousin of Antonius van Phillip and Andries van Phillip, uncle of reincarnated Andries van Phillip, and reincarnated form of sixteenth and seventeenth-century famous diarist Jacobus van Vrederic of the *I Shall Never Let You Go* diaries, also a medical doctor with multiple specialties, and one-of-a-kind specialist in never done before transplant surgeries of the *Vows From The Beyond* diaries

Margriete "Rietje" Jacobus Peters
Sixteenth and seventeenth-century inhabitant, seventeenth-century owner of Kasteel Vrederic, granddaughter of Jacobus van Vrederic and Margriete van Wijck, daughter of Theunis Peters and Griet van Jacobus, wife of Sir Alexander van der Bijl, and inheritor and co-diarist of the fifth diary in the *Kasteel Vrederic* series

Sir Alexander van der Bijl
Knight, sixteenth and seventeenth-century inhabitant, great-grandnephew of Sir Krijn van der Bijl and husband of Margriete "Rietje" Jacobus Peters of the *I Shall Never Let You Go* diaries

Anadhi Newhouse van Phillip
Author, daughter of Dr. Andrew Newhouse and Dr. Gita Shankar Newhouse, granddaughter of Martin Newhouse and Miranda Newhouse, granddaughter of Hari Shankar and Parvati Shankar, wife of Erasmus van Phillip, mother of Jacobus Vrederic van Phillip, aunt and adopted mother of Antonius van Phillip and Andries van Phillip, grandmother of reincarnated Andries van Phillip, and reincarnated form of sixteenth-century Mahalt of the *Vows From The Beyond* diaries

Erasmus van Phillip
World-renowned painter, twenty-first-century owner of Kasteel Vrederic, son of Greta van Phillip, descendant of the van Vrederic family, husband of Anadhi Newhouse van Phillip, father of Jacobus Vrederic van Phillip, uncle and adopted father of Antonius van Phillip and Andries van Phillip, grandfather of reincarnated Andries van Phillip, and reincarnated form of sixteenth-century Johannes van Vrederic of the *Vows From The Beyond* diaries

Antonius van Phillip
World-renowned painter, son of Petrus van Phillip and Giada Berlusconi van Phillip, nephew and adopted son of Erasmus van Phillip and Anadhi Newhouse van Phillip, twin brother of Andries van Phillip, cousin and adopted brother of Jacobus Vrederic van Phillip, husband of Katelijne Snaaijer, and

father of reincarnated Andries van Phillip of the *Vows From The Beyond* diaries

Katelijne Snaaijer   Wife of Antonius van Phillip, mother of reincarnated Andries van Phillip, and stepdaughter of Ghileyn Snaaijer of the *Vows From The Beyond* diaries

Andries van Phillip   Son of Petrus van Phillip and Giada Berlusconi van Phillip, nephew and adopted son of Erasmus van Phillip and Anadhi Newhouse van Phillip, twin brother of Antonius van Phillip, cousin and adopted brother of Jacobus Vrederic van Phillip, and deceased yet reincarnated as son of Antonius van Phillip and Katelijne Snaaijer of the *Vows From The Beyond* diaries

Theunis Peters   Legendary spirit of Kasteel Vrederic, sixteenth-century inhabitant, honorable soldier, husband of Griet van Jacobus, father of Margriete "Rietje" Jacobus Peters, and son-in-law of Jacobus van Vrederic and Margriete van Wijck of the *I Shall Never Let You Go* diaries

Griet van Jacobus   Legendary spirit of Kasteel Vrederic, sixteenth-century inhabitant, daughter of Jacobus van Vrederic and Margriete van Wijck, wife of Theunis Peters, and mother of Margriete "Rietje" Jacobus Peters of the *I Shall Never Let You Go* diaries

Jacobus van Vrederic	Sixteenth and seventeenth-century owner of Kasteel Vrederic, Protestant preacher, son of Johannes van Vrederic and Mahalt, husband of Margriete van Wijck, father of Griet van Jacobus, grandfather of Margriete "Rietje" Jacobus Peters, and the original diarist of the *I Shall Never Let You Go* diaries
Margriete van Wijck	Sixteenth and seventeenth-century inhabitant, beloved wife of Jacobus van Vrederic, mother of Griet van Jacobus, and grandmother of Margriete "Rietje" Jacobus Peters of the *I Shall Never Let You Go* diaries
Dr. Margriete van Achthoven	Cardiologist, reincarnated form of sixteenth and seventeenth-century Margriete van Wijck, and the twin flame of the reincarnated Dr. Jacobus Vrederic van Phillip of the *Vows From The Beyond* diaries
Aunt Marinda	Sixteenth and seventeenth-century inhabitant, and spiritual seer of the *I Shall Never Let You Go* diaries and of the *Vows From The Beyond* diaries
Bertelmeeus van der Berg	Sixteenth and seventeenth-century inhabitant, caretaker of Kasteel Vrederic, and non-blood related uncle of Jacobus van Vrederic of the *I Shall Never Let You Go* diaries
Ghileyn Snaaijer	Stepfather of Katelijne Snaaijer, and Protestant preacher of the *Vows From The Beyond* diaries

Miranda Newhouse "Grandmother" — Seeker, paternal grandmother of Anadhi Newhouse, mother of Dr. Andrew Newhouse, wife of Martin Newhouse, and descendant of Bertelmeeus van der Berg of the *Vows From The Beyond* diaries

Parvati Shankar "Nani" — Maternal grandmother of Anadhi Newhouse, mother of Dr. Gita Shankar Newhouse, and wife of Hari Shankar of the *Vows From The Beyond* diaries

Greta van Phillip — Mother of Erasmus van Phillip and descendant of van Vrederic family of the *Vows From The Beyond* diaries

Griete van Phillip — Aunt of Erasmus van Phillip and descendant of van Vrederic family of the *Vows From The Beyond* diaries

Grietje van Phillip — Aunt of Erasmus van Phillip and descendant of van Vrederic family of the *Vows From The Beyond* diaries

Matthias van Phillip — Cousin of Erasmus van Phillip and descendant of van Vrederic family of the *Vows From The Beyond* diaries

Petrus van Phillip — Cousin of Erasmus van Phillip and descendant of van Vrederic family of the *Vows From The Beyond* diaries

Sir Krijn van der Bijl — Knight, and great-granduncle of Sir Alexander van der Bijl of the *I Shall Never Let You Go* diaries

Johannes van Vrederic — Sixteenth-century inhabitant, original owner of Kasteel Vrederic, husband of Mahalt, and father of Jacobus van

ANN MARIE RUBY

Vrederic of the *I Shall Never Let You Go* diaries

Mahalt Sixteenth-century inhabitant, wife of Johannes van Vrederic, and mother of Jacobus van Vrederic of the *I Shall Never Let You Go* diaries

238

GLOSSARY

Get acquainted with some Dutch and Hindi terms, and places in the Netherlands and India that were used in this book.

Amsterdam   Capital city of the Netherlands.

Catholicism   Christian faith that follows the Roman Catholic Church led by the Pope.

Chamber Pot   This pot was used as an indoor toilet prior to flushing toilets.

Dengue   A fever that is caused by mosquito bites from infected mosquitoes.

Dreams   REM (rapid eye movement) cycle is when a sleeping body can travel through their dreams. Proven scientifically dreams can occur and people do travel during their dreams however their bodies do not leave their places. Religions have mainly come through dreams. More information on dreams can be found in the book *Eternal Truth: The Tunnel Of Light* by Ann Marie Ruby.

Dutch   Term refers to both the language spoken and the people in the Netherlands.

Dutch Eighty Years' War The Netherlands during 1568 through 1648 was involved in this war. This was the Dutch war of independence involving modern-day the Netherlands, Belgium and Luxembourg in opposition to the ruling of Philip II of Spain. More information on the Dutch Eighty Years' War can be found in the book *The Netherlands: Land Of My Dreams* by Ann Marie Ruby.

Dutch Resistance Army During the Dutch Eighty Years' War, this group was created initially led by the Father of the Fatherland (the Netherlands), William the Silent, to fight against the army of King Philip II of Spain.

Gallows A place commonly known where witches were hung to their death.

India Officially the Republic of India, country located in South Asia, and the second most populated country in the world.

Kasteel Vrederic Castle Vrederic is the home of the van Vrederic family in the *Kasteel Vrederic* series, spanning from the sixteenth century through the present.

Naarden City in the province of North Holland in the Netherlands.

Nani Maternal grandmother in Hindi.

New Delhi Capital of India.

North Holland	Province in the Netherlands.
North Sea	Sea off the Atlantic Ocean which expands across different countries including the Netherlands.
Oma	Grandmother in Dutch.
Opa	Grandfather in Dutch.
Oudewater	Town and municipality in the province of Utrecht.
Protestantism	Christian faith that resulted after sixteenth-century Reformation in Europe.
Reincarnation/Rebirth	Belief system of a lot of people worldwide such as Buddhism, Hinduism, Jainism, Sikhism, and more. Today science can't disprove reincarnation. Also a lot of people have given proof of their rebirth. More information on reincarnation can be found in the book *Eternal Truth: The Tunnel Of Light* by Ann Marie Ruby.
Scheveningen	Seaside resort and fishing port on the North Sea in The Hague, the Netherlands.
Sleep Paralysis	A stage that happens to a huge population of people around the globe. There is no research as to why it happens yet its existence is proven mythologically and scientifically.

Soul Family People who are in various lifetimes born in the same house, neighborhood, or around one another. More information on soul families can be found in the book *Eternal Truth: The Tunnel Of Light* by Ann Marie Ruby.

Spaniards Members of the Spanish army who fought for the King of Spain.

Stakes A place where witches were burned to death.

The Hague Political capital of the Netherlands within the province of South Holland.

Tunnel Of Light Scientifically it is known as the NDE (near-death experience) tunnel. More information on the tunnel of light can be found in the book *Eternal Truth: The Tunnel Of Light* by Ann Marie Ruby.

Twin Flames Research has shown twin flames can survive as individuals yet are complete as one. More information on twin flames can be found in the book *Eternal Truth: The Tunnel Of Light* by Ann Marie Ruby.

Weighing House One of the famous weighing houses across Europe is in Oudewater, the Netherlands where people found their freedom when weighed and proved they actually did weigh and so could not be light enough to fly on broomsticks, proving their innocence. More information on the weighing house in Oudewater can be found in the book *Everblooming: Through The Twelve Provinces Of The Netherlands* by Ann Marie Ruby.

Witch Hunts   A tribunal, heretical, and shameful time for the world, as innocent women or men who were thought to be witches or warlocks, because someone might have just accused the person or the person could have had some special gift.

MESSAGE FROM THE AUTHOR

"Love withstands time. Time leaves us as she crosses our door. Love leaves us with sweet and sour memories, as she crosses even time. For even when all but ends, love survives through eternal vows."

Dear Readers,

In this book, you the reader will see how a grandfather defies time and tide to prove love lives on even beyond time. For he returns to the sixteenth century from the twenty-first century as he keeps his vows from the beyond. He does not forget, "Opa's heart beats Rietje."

He proves to all love is a sacred promise given and found between souls. It is not always that love is found between twin flames because what about the connection between a grandfather and his beloved granddaughter? In this book, you will see how love is defined in different categories. The connection between families, a father and a son, a mother and her sons, a grandfather and his beloved granddaughter, and what about brothers? So why don't you all travel through this book and my *Kasteel Vrederic* series? Here you will find that love stories are created between twin flames yet continue throughout the family tree where love begins and ends only as it begins again.

Life gives us love and joy to walk and deal with throughout time. Yet sometimes in life we all need a break where we can forget all of our troubles and just feel free. Maybe some of us can take a break and go to the park, or maybe to the beach, or maybe turn the television sets on and watch a movie.

I feel like my biggest pleasure and break comes from opening a book where I can escape to and through. This is why I have created my *Kasteel Vrederic* series for all of you. Here you can actually get a complete package vacation. You will find yourself a family you too want to be a part of and an infinite passionate romance where you too would say this is real love. You will see the bond between a family.

These books will lift your spirits up as you will always know when you feel lonely and lost, all you have to do is just open the pages of any of these books, be rejuvenated, and feel better. I hope you have read all of the Kasteel Vrederic diaries. These diaries have come to all of us as inspiration to and from the sixteenth century through the twenty-first century. Based in Naarden, the Netherlands where a noble Dutchman had started his famous diaries as a gift left for his granddaughter Rietje, and all others who also needed some inspiration from a sixteenth-century diarist.

Come and become a daughter, a granddaughter, a mother, a son, a father, or a brother as you become a beloved member of this family. A man fights to keep his family through the war-ridden country. Come and see how he takes even death and makes life a blessed journey through his diaries.

The diaries had started in the sixteenth century during the Dutch Eighty Years' War. Then their lives involved the unjust witch hunts that had gone wild within Europe and all across the world. A country ripped apart by war also had a man fighting to save his child, his wife, and family as he fought his own war, during the unjust witch burnings and knew he must stand up and fight for the witches as no one else would.

The family members crossed time and landed in the twenty-first century where they had to gain faith in reincarnation and dreams to realize love and lovers can actually cross time to be with one another. Who says if you can't unite in one life, you can never unite? For true lovers rise like the rising phoenix from ashes and again try to unite with only one another.

In the twenty-first century, this family again faces separation, death, and murder mystery. To unite again with one another, they must take upon the miraculous door of dreams and believe in miracles. Born blind, a twin must avenge murders happening across the globe. Here a blind son of Kasteel Vrederic awakens and finds out he was not left alone to deal with this situation as he had his Kasteel Vrederic family members who too walked with him. He had fought the prophecy that foretold he must fall in love with a dead woman to make sure she is alive. Yet how does he achieve this goal? Well in the Kasteel Vrederic family home, anything is possible and nothing is impossible.

Then again we travel to the past as when and where a family member of Kasteel Vrederic needs a helping hand, all the family members unite and even time travel to make sure their family member is safe. For what happens if this family member is not saved? Then all the future generations too would be no more. So here we watch how a family together saves the family tree forever.

Now all of you must walk with me and go ahead in the future where again Jacobus Vrederic van Phillip must find his twin flame Margriete and recognize her. For this time, the Kasteel Vrederic family members are uniting to bring back honor to the child who once was known as the forbidden daughter of Kasteel Vrederic. So come and journey through another book in the *Kasteel Vrederic* series where the family members will walk through a paranormal romance mystery, where an infinite love story is reborn while they must all bring back home their daughter all had called, *Forbidden Daughter Of Kasteel Vrederic: Vows From The Beyond*, releasing soon.

All of these books will bring back faith in true love. Love does not mean always happily ever after, as life has death, birth, and sorrows as well as happiness all blanketed into one. Yet we all want to escape to another world where we can all feel like we too belong in this world. Here everyone feels like family. Here everyone is welcome. Here you too can feel right at home.

So to forget all of your troubles and feel like you are on a permanent vacation where you can just be in your own home and still be in the Netherlands with the Kasteel Vrederic family members, why don't you all walk into the world of Kasteel Vrederic? Here, yes, you will cry with them. You will laugh with them and always at the end come out feeling it's all going to be just all right.

Come and be a member of this family just by reading all the books in this series. For remember, after reading this series you too shall believe in the door of miracles, the door of reincarnation, and the door of dreams, which shall actually take you to a blessed home everyone knows as Kasteel Vrederic.

Now let us travel through the personal diaries of the inhabitants of Kasteel Vrederic. Original copies of these diaries are, however, kept with love and care in the blessed library of Kasteel Vrederic. For you though, here is a short glimpse into the complete series in order of reading.

BOOK ONE:

Eternally Beloved: I Shall Never Let You Go

This book introduces you to Kasteel Vrederic through the first diary of the famous diarist Jacobus van Vrederic. He walks you through his sad love story and goes through the love story of his daughter Griet van Jacobus and the brave soldier Theunis Peter. Based during the Dutch Eighty Years' War in the sixteenth century.

BOOK TWO:

Evermore Beloved: I Shall Never Let You Go

Here you walk through the amazing love story of Jacobus van Vrederic and his beloved wife Margriete van Wijck, where we get to meet Jacobus's beloved granddaughter, baby Rietje. Based during the witch trials and the Dutch Eighty Years' War in the sixteenth and seventeenth centuries.

BOOK THREE:

Be My Destiny: Vows From The Beyond

This book takes you through reincarnation and the blessed door of dreams. Here infinite twin flames Erasmus van Phillip, a twenty-first-century descendant of Jacobus van Vrederic and the reincarnated father of Jacobus van Vrederic, is reborn again to find and unite with his forever twin flame, Anadhi Newhouse, also the reincarnated mother of Jacobus van Vrederic. Find out how their son reunites them through the twenty-first century and takes them back to Kasteel Vrederic.

BOOK FOUR:

Heart Beats Your Name: Vows From The Beyond

Here you will get introduced to a blind son of the Kasteel Vrederic family, the nephew and adopted son of Erasmus van Phillip and Anadhi Newhouse van Phillip. In this paranormal thriller, you will see how Dr. Jacobus Vrederic van Phillip, the biological son of Erasmus and Anadhi, guides his brother to unite with his pronounced dead wife, while trying to solve her murder mystery. A paranormal book where everyone realizes family members are bound with one another throughout time.

BOOK FIVE:

Entranced Beloved: I Shall Never Let You Go
Twenty-first-century Dr. Jacobus Vrederic van Phillip must return to the seventeenth-century Kasteel Vrederic, as he realizes his beloved granddaughter is missing and must be rescued for the inhabitants of *Vows From The Beyond* to even exist. This can only be done through the miraculous hands of the famous twenty-first-century physician. So here we go, Dr. Jacobus must travel time and go back to the *I Shall Never Let You Go* diaries. Walk back and get reacquainted with the seventeenth-century Kasteel Vrederic family members with Dr. Jacobus as he meets his sixteenth-century self, Jacobus van Vrederic. Margriete "Rietje" Jacobus Peters and Sir Alexander van der Bijl's love story is

written and retold by the twenty-first-century famous physician, Dr. Jacobus from the *Vows From The Beyond* diaries.

-Ann Marie Ruby

ABOUT THE AUTHOR

"Meet Ann Marie Ruby from Seattle, Washington. This is her story."

Ann Marie Ruby was born into a diplomatic family for which she had the privilege of traveling the world. This upbringing made the whole world her one family. She never saw a country as a foreign country yet as a neighbor who was there for her as she would be there for them. After all, isn't that what families do for one another?

Ann Marie became an author as she started to place her chosen words into the pages of her diaries. She knew she must collect all her thoughts and produce them into different diaries. Each diary became her different books.

Ann Marie's life goal is not to just write something but only what she believes in. So all her thoughts and words remained within the pages of her diaries until she realized it was time she must share them with you. Otherwise, she felt selfish and knew that was not her characteristic as she lives for everyone, not just for herself.

INTERNATIONAL #1 BESTSELLING AUTHOR:

Ann Marie became an international number-one bestselling author of eighteen books. Alongside being a full-time author, she loves to write articles on her website where she can have a better connection with all of you. Ann Marie, a dream psychic, became a blogger and a humanitarian only because she believes in you and herself as a complete, honest, and open family.

PERSONAL:

Ann Marie is an American who grew up in Brisbane, Australia. She resided in the Washington, D.C. area, but later settled in Seattle, Washington. In her spare time when she is not writing books, she loves to meditate, pray, listen to music, cook, and write blog posts.

BESTSELLING:

Ann Marie's books have placed her on top 100 bestselling charts in various countries including the Netherlands, United States, United Kingdom, Canada, and Germany. In 2020, she became a household name as her books began to consistently rank #1 on multiple bestselling charts. *The Netherlands: Land Of My Dreams* and *Everblooming: Through The Twelve Provinces Of The Netherlands*, both became overnight number-one bestsellers in the United States.

In 2020, *The Netherlands: Land Of My Dreams* also became a bestseller in the Netherlands and Canada, consistently becoming #1 on various lists and one of the top selling books on Amazon NL. *Everblooming: Through The Twelve Provinces Of The Netherlands* became #37 on the Netherlands top 100 bestselling Amazon books chart which includes all books from all genres. Ann Marie's other books have also made various top 100 bestselling lists and received multiple accolades including *Eternal Truth: The Tunnel Of Light* which was named as one of eight thought-provoking books by women.

ROMANCE FICTION:

Ann Marie's *Kasteel Vrederic* series was written in a diary fashion. She has always kept a diary herself, so she thought her characters too could keep a diary. All of their diaries became individual books yet collectively, they are a part of a family, the Kasteel Vrederic family.

OTHER BOOKS:

All of Ann Marie's nonfiction and fiction books are available globally. You can take a look at short descriptions about the books at the end of this book.

THE NETHERLANDS:

Ann Marie revealed why many of her books revolve around the Netherlands, sharing that as a dream psychic, she had seen the historical past of a country in her dreams and was later able to place a name to the country. This is described in detail in *Spiritual Lighthouse: The Dream Diaries Of Ann Marie Ruby* and *The Netherlands: Land Of My Dreams* where she also wrote about her plans to eventually move to the Netherlands.

Ann Marie has received letters on behalf of His Majesty King Willem-Alexander and Her Majesty Queen Máxima of the Netherlands after they received her books *The Netherlands: Land Of My Dreams* and *Everblooming: Through The Twelve Provinces Of The Netherlands.* Additionally, Ann Marie has received letters on behalf of His Excellency Mark Rutte, the Prime Minister of the Netherlands for her books.

WRITING:

Ann Marie also is acclaimed globally as one of the top voices in the spiritual space, however, she is recognized for her writing abilities published across many genres namely spirituality, lifestyle, inspirational quotations, poetry, fiction, romance, history, travel, social awareness, and more. Her writing style is hailed by critics and readers alike as making readers feel as though they have made a friend.

FOLLOW THE AUTHOR:

Now as you have found her book, why don't you and Ann Marie become friends? Join her and become a part of her global family. Ann Marie shall always give you books which you will read and then find yourself as a part of her book family.

For more information about Ann Marie Ruby, any one of her books, or to read her blog posts and articles, subscribe to her website, www.annmarieruby.com.

Follow Ann Marie Ruby on social media:
Twitter: @AnnahMariahRuby
Facebook: @TheAnnMarieRuby
Instagram: @Ann_Marie_Ruby
Pinterest: @TheAnnMarieRuby

BOOKS BY THE AUTHOR

INSPIRATIONAL QUOTATIONS SERIES:

This series includes four books of original quotations and one omnibus edition.

Spiritual Travelers:
Life's Journey From The Past
To The Present
For The Future

Spiritual
Messages:
From A Bottle

Spiritual Journey:
Life's Eternal Blessings

Spiritual
Inspirations:
Sacred Words
Of Wisdom

Omnibus edition contains all four books of original quotations.

Spiritual Ark:
The Enchanted Journey Of Timeless
Quotations

SPIRITUAL SONGS SERIES:

This series includes two original spiritual prayer books.

SPIRITUAL SONGS: LETTERS FROM MY CHEST

When there was no hope, I found hope within these sacred words of prayers, I but call songs. Within this book, I have for you, 100 very sacred prayers.

SPIRITUAL SONGS II: BLESSINGS FROM A SACRED SOUL

Prayers are but the sacred doors to an individual's enlightenment. This book has 123 prayers for all humans with humanity.

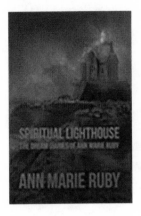

SPIRITUAL LIGHTHOUSE: THE DREAM DIARIES OF ANN MARIE RUBY

Do you believe in dreams? For within each individual dream, there is a hidden message and a miracle interlinked. Learn the spiritual, scientific, religious, and philosophical aspects of dreams. Walk with me as you travel through forty nights, through the pages of my book.

THE WORLD HATE CRISIS: THROUGH THE EYES OF A DREAM PSYCHIC

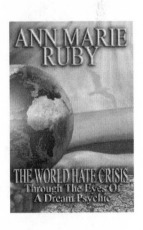

Humans have walked into an age where humanity now is being questioned as hate crimes have reached a catastrophic amount. Let us in union stop this crisis. Pick up my book and see if you too could join me in this fight.

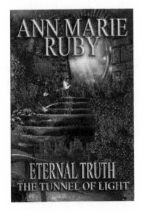

ETERNAL TRUTH: THE TUNNEL OF LIGHT

Within this book, travel with me through the doors of birth, death, reincarnation, true soulmates and twin flames, dreams, miracles, and the end of time.

THE NETHERLANDS: LAND OF MY DREAMS

Oh the sacred travelers, be like the mystical river and journey through this blessed land through my book. Be the flying bird of wisdom and learn about a land I call, Heaven on Earth.

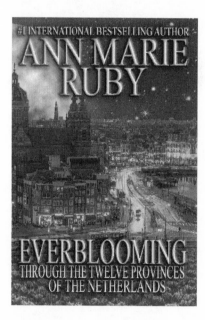

EVERBLOOMING: THROUGH THE TWELVE PROVINCES OF THE NETHERLANDS

Original poetry and hand-picked tales are bound together in this keepsake book. Come travel with me as I take you through the lives of the Dutch past.

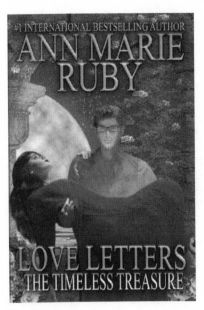

LOVE LETTERS: THE TIMELESS TREASURE

Fifty original timeless treasured love poems are presented with individual illustrations describing each poem.

KASTEEL VREDERIC SERIES:

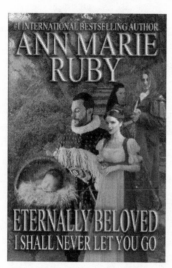

ETERNALLY BELOVED: I SHALL NEVER LET YOU GO

Travel time to the sixteenth century where Jacobus van Vrederic, a beloved lover and father, surmounts time and tide to find the vanished love of his life. On his pursuit, Jacobus discovers secrets that will alter his life evermore. He travels through the Eighty Years' War-ravaged country, the Netherlands as he takes the vow, even if separated by a breath, "Eternally beloved, I shall never let you go."

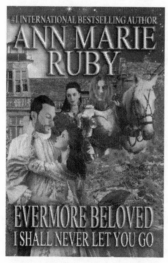

EVERMORE BELOVED: I SHALL NEVER LET YOU GO

Jacobus van Vrederic returns with the devoted spirits of Kasteel Vrederic. A knight and a seer also join him on a quest to find his lost evermore beloved. They journey through a war-ravaged country, the Netherlands, to stop another war which was brewing silently in his land, called the witch hunts. Time was his enemy as he must defeat time and tide to find his evermore beloved wife alive.

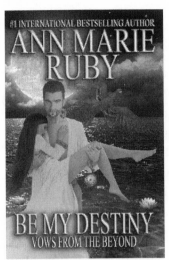

BE MY DESTINY: VOWS FROM THE BEYOND

Fighting their biggest enemy destiny, twin flames Erasmus van Phillip and Anadhi Newhouse are reborn over and over again only to lose the battle to destiny. Find out if through the helping hands of sacred spirits of the sixteenth century, these eternal twin flames are finally able to unite in the twenty-first century, as they say, "Reincarnation is a blessing if only you are mine."

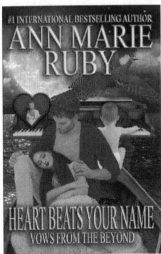

HEART BEATS YOUR NAME: VOWS FROM THE BEYOND

While one is sleepless, the other twin flame is sleeping eternally. Now how does Antonius van Phillip awaken his twin flame Katelijne Snaaijer from beyond Earth, and solve a murder mystery, she is the only witness to yet also a victim of? Find out how the musical sound of heartbeats guide him to his sleeping beloved while he solves the mystery sleepless.

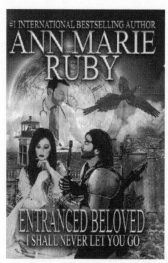

ENTRANCED BELOVED: I SHALL NEVER LET YOU GO

The pages of Margriete "Rietje" Jacobus Peters's love story from her diary slowly go missing from the library of Kasteel Vrederic. The twenty-first-century descendants fighting death and time must travel back in time to save their ancestors and their beloved Kasteel Vrederic. Traveling through the tunnel of light, the family of the twenty-first century must save the seventeenth-century twin flames. Rietje and her beloved twin flame Sir Alexander van der Bijl must create another paranormal, magical, historical, romantic diary for the dynasty to even exist.

Coming Soon

FORBIDDEN DAUGHTER OF KASTEEL VREDERIC: VOWS FROM THE BEYOND

FORBIDDEN DAUGHTER OF KASTEEL VREDERIC: VOWS FROM THE BEYOND

The sixth book in this series is coming soon.

Made in the USA
Las Vegas, NV
28 December 2023

83649541R00162